RETURN TO SUNSHINE COTTAGE

HOPING TO FIND LOVE AGAIN

BERNICE BLOOM

"This tale will amaze and delight you; it will warm your heart."
"Love, tenderness, joy and beauty. Bernie Bloom has it all in this gem."

FOREWORD

Hello,

Welcome to the world of Sunshine Cottage. This is the first novel in a six-book series about the gorgeous Lopez sisters who live in a beautiful fishing village called Cove Bay near Salcombe in south Devon.

The Lopez sisters are very different - there's Sophia, the beauty in the pack. Then there's Emma, who is sports-mad and loves drinking beers with the boys; Isabella, the hairdresser obsessed with losing weight; and Lisa - the star of this first book - a sensitive soul who works as a gardener and loves the outdoors. She is returning to Cove Bay after suffering a massive heartbreak.

The sisters still live at home in a beautiful little yellow cottage on the beach.

As the books open, things have become very interesting in Cove Bay because a new rugby team has moved into the area. It means there are lots of very fit, handsome men wandering around. It's perfect for our single sisters...or is it?

Things are never smooth sailing with the women - there are tears, heartbreak, love, joy and thrills aplenty. It's like Little Women for the modern age (with lots of romance thrown in).

I hope you enjoy this book and the others in the series – each is devoted to a different woman in Cove Bay.

FOREWORD

Lots of love,
Bernie x

MEET THE LOPEZ FAMILY

- LISA is a romantic at heart and wants to spend her life immersed in the beauty of flowers and plants and with the man she loves. When that man breaks her heart, she is devastated and swears she'll never love again...until a handsome sports coach starts paying her lots of attention.
- SOPHIA is a glamorous blonde - the most attractive of the girls, always beautifully dressed and with a spectacular figure. She loves getting all dressed up and attracts attention wherever she goes, but will she ever meet someone who loves her for who she is rather than what she looks like?
- EMMA is the comedian of the group. She is naturally pretty, smiley and funny, and she doesn't care at all what she looks like. She has no ambition to succeed in life; she just wants wanted to hang out with friends and work in the local sports bar. Her sisters despair of her ever meeting anyone.
- ISABELLA is a hairdresser...she is completely down to earth, a little bit chubby and always worried about her

weight. She would love to meet someone but is convinced that being overweight stops men from being interested.

- GEORGINA is mum! She's a retired teacher who's enjoying spending more time with her daughters now she doesn't have to work.
- DONALD is dad: a retired oyster fisherman who moved to Cove Bay from Emerald Isle when he met Georgina.
- CHARLIE is a friend of the sisters, so not, technically speaking, a Lopez family member, but she comes to stay with them and feels like part of the family

The family lives at Sunshine Cottage. Lisa works at Suffolk Manor. Isabella and Sophia work on Top Street & Emma works at the rugby club.

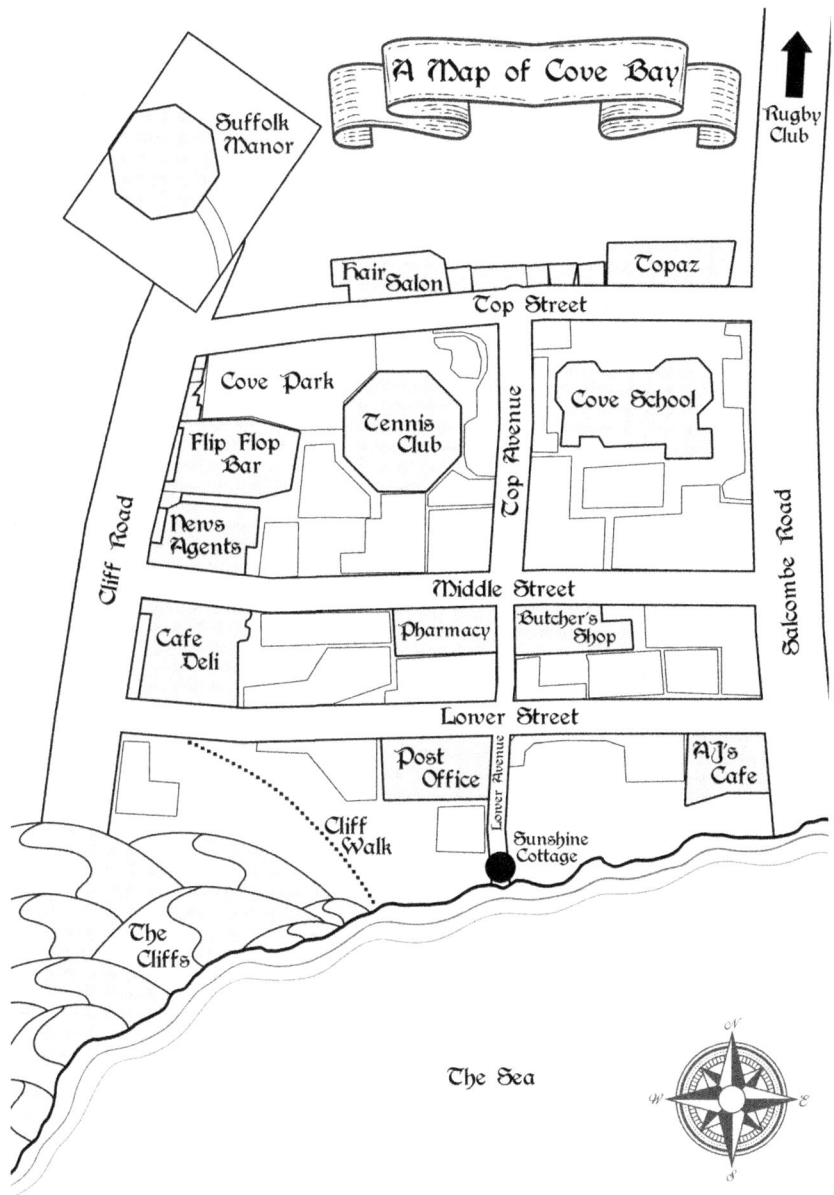

CHAPTER 1

*L*isa Lopez snuggled into her seat and smiled to herself. She was going home, and she couldn't be happier.

A thrill of delight and excitement quivered through her as she buckled her seatbelt and pulled the soft blanket around her shoulders. Partying in Edinburgh for two months had been great fun, but she'd missed her family; it would be great to get home to her three crazy sisters, her mum and dad, and to Sunshine Cottage - their beautiful, ramshackle, pale yellow cottage on the beach.

The only thing that worried her, terrified her, in fact, was seeing Peter. She was bound to bump into him.

Oh God, even the thought of him made her feel like screaming.

Lisa had been born in Sunshine Cottage and had spent all her life in Cove Bay, a little fishing village right next to Salcombe in south Devon. It was such a beautiful little place, nestled in the rocks with pastel-coloured houses dotted along the beachfront and turquoise waters that twisted into foam-peaked waves, carrying the white sails of dozens of boats out to sea. It was where she'd scabbed her knees while learning to ride a bike on the dirt tracks through the woods and where she'd developed her fascination with gardening and grown a love of plants and flowers that remained with her and had grown inside her over the years. It was also where she'd fallen in love, completely, madly and deeply, and had her heart broken with such velocity that she'd had to flee to Edinburgh to recover.

Lisa tried to shrug off the memory of Peter - the warmth of him, the sight and sound of him, and the day she'd finally caught him out.

That part of her life was over now. She'd moved on. But, my goodness, it was hard.

As she felt herself welling up, she tried to concentrate on how much fun it would be to see her family. The lovely thing about their home was that she and her sisters had all moved back and lived in the house where they had grown up. They were in their twenties and thirties now, with jobs, friends and busy lives, but for a variety of reasons - men, money, work - they had been forced to return to the family home. And it was wonderful.

Her father sometimes moaned about it: "Will I always be surrounded by women? Will I ever escape the tights and lipsticks?" But they all knew he didn't mean it. He loved them, and they loved him, and now she longed to be back with them, waking up to the sounds of the ocean and the sight of the sandy beach right outside her window. She wanted to hear nothing but the waves as she walked over the rocks. She wanted to feel the breeze waking her up and restoring her sanity.

"Excuse me," said a deep voice, breaking her out of her daydream. Standing next to her was a large and scruffily-dressed man clutching a pile of tatty-looking sports magazines. He wore an old rugby shirt and didn't look as if he'd shaved for months. He indicated her novel, lying in his seat.

"Sorry," she said, moving it as he dropped his magazines and reached down to pick them up, straining and swearing to himself with the effort before sitting down heavily. He knocked his arm into her as he pushed his magazines into the seat pocket in front of him. He fussed about making himself comfortable, stretching, adjusting and forcing her to curl into the corner of her seat, as far away from him as she could get.

Just her luck! She'd opted to fly back to Devon instead of getting the train; thinking is would be less trouble; she had wanted to sit back, read her book and relax on the journey. Instead, she was next to this loutish bloke who was too big for his seat and couldn't keep still. And she would be stuck here for the next hour. He shuffled around, removing his jacket, then reached into his pocket to remove his phone and turn it off before realising there was a message on it. He played the message, switched off the phone, and then finally, *finally*, he sat still.

"Would you put on your seat belt, please?" asked the flight attendant.

"Must I?" he asked, rubbing his face with his hands.

Lisa watched in astonishment. Had he never flown before? Was there anyone in the world who didn't know that you had to wear a seat belt?

"Everyone must wear seat belts. Aviation regulations" said the flight attendant. "Even you, I'm afraid."

"OK, OK," he muttered, removing his baseball cap and tucking it into the seat pocket. The flight attendant hovered, and Lisa distracted herself with the book in her lap as he huffed and puffed beside her. She leaned her head against the cool glass while he made an absolute show of pulling the seat belt out and loosening it by shaking it. He knocked into her several times without apologising once. He swore loudly to himself as he tucked his scarf into the seat pocket in front of him, watching as the end trailed out onto the floor. "Scotland Rugby," it read. There's a surprise!

Lisa had no interest in sports. She'd never cared about them or particularly understood them. The sportsmen she'd come across were loutish and loud, and it was impossible to imagine how they could become so excited by men running around hitting balls, catching balls and throwing balls.

She knew this was not how most people felt. Indeed, it was not how her three sisters felt. They seemed unduly interested in sport recently and were all buoyed by the fact that a new sports team had moved to the area. They'd written several letters to tell Lisa how great the team was. It had moved to the area from Exeter, thanks to some issue with the stadium in the city. Now the team was settled in Salcombe, less than a mile from Sunshine Cottage. Lisa had no interest at all. Now this man confirmed all her worst fears about sportspeople. She turned back to her novel.

"Is it any good?" asked the man.

"Sorry?"

"The book…is it any good?"

"Yes, it is."

He looked at her through half-closed eyes, grinning a little. He had lovely brown eyes with thick eyelashes. He had a dimple in the middle of his chin and was kind of cute despite his scruffiness and loudness, or would be if he learned to shave.

Lisa looked back down at the page, but she could feel the guy staring at her. She didn't want to have a conversation with him. She just wanted to read.

"I'm Matt," he said suddenly.

"Hi. Lisa," she replied, and they shook hands.

"Did you enjoy your time in Edinburgh?" he asked.

"I did. It's a beautiful city," she said.

"Did you get the chance to see the castle?"

"Yes, I went a few times. I particularly loved the views from the top of the Lang stairs. That was amazing."

"Oh, me too. There's something about those stairs that gets to me, and the views are awesome."

Lisa smiled and went back to her book. He was right about the stairs; they had a magical appeal in all their old-world cragginess. There had been some real highlights on her trip. She went back to her book, half reading and half letting her mind wander back to her time in the Scottish capital.

"You look like you're a million miles away."

"Yes, just reading," she said, smiling at Matt but looking down at the pages in front of her.

"You're a mighty slow reader. You haven't turned a page yet."

"I didn't realise I was being monitored," she replied. Why couldn't he just leave her alone?

He smiled. He had a good smile; she had to give him that.

"No, no. No monitoring. I'll leave you alone."

Lisa turned back to her book, eager to while away the hours until the plane began its descent into Exeter airport.

SHE HAD MANAGED to get through the whole flight without speaking to anyone. When the plane touched down, Matt began to gather up all his things, bending to retrieve his scarf and hat and pulling his magazines out from the seat pocket in front of him. He seemed much more animated now, much chattier and happier than when he'd first arrived on the plane.

"I'm glad that's over," he said. "Sorry if I was annoying. I hate flying…absolutely hate it. I'm horrible on flights. You drew the short straw when they sat you next to me. Apologies."

"No problem," she said, relieved to be home.

"I've got a car meeting me if you need a lift anywhere?"

"I'm fine," said Lisa, smiling at him and thanking him for the gesture. "My sisters are coming to pick me up, so I'll be OK."

"Sisters? Do they all look like you?"

"I guess so," Lisa replied, though the truth was that they weren't really like her at all. There was Sophia, the glamorous blonde who was the most attractive of them—always beautifully dressed (she worked in Cove Bay's finest clothes shop, so she had heavy discounts!) She was like Cameron Diaz—a spectacular figure, big blue eyes and always immaculate.

Emma couldn't be more different; she was naturally pretty, smiley and funny—the comedian of the group and a sports nut, Matt would probably have lots in common with her. She didn't care what she looked like and just wanted to hang out with her friends all the time. She worked in the friendly local cafe when Lisa left for Scotland but now worked at the bar of the new sports club.

Finally, there was Isabella, a hairdresser—completely down-to-earth, a little bit chubby and always worried about her weight; she was the world's chattiest person. Once she got you into the salon chair, she'd talk at you until your ears bled! By the time she'd finished styling your locks, you'd know everything about everyone who lived in Cove Bay.

Lisa didn't know how people would describe her...perhaps as the kind and vulnerable one. She was always getting upset and worrying about other people. Or they might describe her as a pushover. And, if they did, they'd probably be right. She knew she was far too easygoing for her own good. She was happy to go with the flow and do what other people wanted rather than assert herself and make everyone do what she wanted.

Lisa reached for her handbag that was pushed beneath the seat in front of her and pulled out her phone. It was only when she was switching it on, checking her messages and loosening her seatbelt that she realised she had just been complimented. He'd been nice about her. Asking whether her sisters all looked like her had to count as a compliment, didn't it?

She turned to Matt, but he was fiddling with his phone and grunting like a water buffalo as he read through messages that he didn't agree with. He shoved his crumpled magazines into the inside pocket of his jacket, almost tearing them to pieces as he did. Everything about him was so big and male and oversized - crashing and bashing like a hairy hippo.

Perhaps he hadn't meant it as a compliment at all. Perhaps he was just genuinely interested in whether they looked alike.

People were starting to leave the plane, but Matt showed no sign of moving from his seat; he looked through his phone while the queue down the aisle began to move.

"May I get past you?" she asked.

"Sure, sorry." He stood up, banging his head on the overhead lockers and cursing wildly. "After you."

Lisa moved into the line of people exiting the plane and swiftly through to the baggage collection area. She reached into her handbag for her phone while she was waiting for her bag.

"Thank you, thank you, thank you for having me," she wrote to Charlie. "Have safely landed. Tell your lovely brother, Max, that I love him. Can't wait to see you. xxx"

She put her phone away and retrieved her bag before walking through to arrivals. She scanned the crowds, looking for her sisters.

"LISA!!!!"

She heard the girls before she saw them. Emma and Isabella dashed across the concourse, arms outstretched, smiles plastered across their familiar faces, while Sophia, looking as incredibly beautiful as ever, clapped wildly from where she stood.

"I'm afraid these shoes don't do running," she said. "But it's awesome to see you again." Lisa smiled and dropped her bags as they hugged her and stroked her hair, telling her how great she looked. You'd think she'd been away at war or something.

"You look amazing," said Sophia. "My God. How much weight have you lost? You look completely lovely."

"I'm so envious," said Isabella. "I have to move to Edinburgh immediately. I need to know how you've done it. Tell me: what did you do? How much weight have you lost?"

"I've lost about ten pounds, I think." Lisa had no real idea how much she'd lost. A couple of dress sizes, perhaps? The combination of a heartache diet and being out working all day, every day, had meant the weight had fallen off her. She knew Isabella would be heartbroken to hear it, but there was no magic formula, no step-by-step guide to losing weight. She just hadn't eaten very much!

STILL, it was nice to be told she looked lovely by Sophia since the woman herself looked like a supermodel. If she weren't so completely lovely, you could hate her. Today she wore a cream silk shirt tucked into elegant cream trousers. A lovely brown and cream scarf was tied around her neck in an arty twist. Whenever Lisa wore a scarf like that, she looked like an air hostess from the 1950s, but Sophia managed to look like she'd just stepped off a Paris runway.

"Come on, skinny bones, let's go to the car," said Isabella. "I really need to go to Edinburgh. I'm the size of a damn horse."

"No, you're not," chipped in Emma. "A pony, maybe, but not a horse."

"Ha, ha, you're so witty," replied Isabella, but before she could continue, they were interrupted.

"WELL, WELL, WHAT HAVE WE HERE?"

They all spun around at the sound of the man's voice. It was Matt from the aeroplane standing there with his hair standing on end, scarf trailing on the dirty floor and his shirt untucked.

Lisa felt herself blush.

"Meet my sisters," she said, preparing to introduce them, but before she could speak, Emma and Isabella had launched themselves at him and were hugging him affectionately.

"Hi, darling," said Sophia, kissing him on the cheek with trademark restraint.

"So, you guys know one another?" asked Lisa.

"Of course we do. Matt, meet our little sister, Lisa," said Emma.

"We've met," said Matt, looking sideways at Lisa. "In fact, we were sitting next to one another on the flight. I was a nightmare because I'm terrified of flying, so she ignored me completely."

"Sorry," said Lisa, feeling churlish. She hadn't realised he was terrified of flying.

"What an amazing coincidence that you met on the plane," said Emma. "Are you going to come back to our place? Mom will have hot chocolate and cake ready for us."

"I won't, actually. I've got a ton of stuff to do tonight and training first thing. But thanks for inviting me, and say hi to your mom."

"You know my mom?" said Lisa.

"I know your whole family," said Matt. "And now that I've worked out who you are, I can tell you I know a hell of a lot about you too…"

CHAPTER 2

*L*isa woke up, stretched and smiled as a feeling of warm familiarity snaked through her body. She was tucked up in her bed, and it felt beautiful. Nothing, no amount of travelling or exploring, could replace the sheer delight of returning home.

As she lay there and looked around, her surroundings helped her feelings of joy considerably. She had the best bedroom in the house, the only downstairs one; it had creaky patio doors that opened onto a very rustic wooden deck, which slipped seamlessly onto the beach. She'd been given this bedroom by default; the others were all full because her mom and dad hadn't necessarily planned on having another child. So, when she came along they turned the downstairs storeroom into a fifth bedroom. Lisa adored it. She always had. The floor was wooden and rough beneath her feet, but she'd stopped her parents from smoothing and varnishing it because she didn't want to lose the authentic look of it. She just had to remember to wear her huge, fluffy slippers in there. Her curtains and the bedspread were cream. She was usually the sort of person who loved bright colours, but she'd stuck with cream - it seemed to work, somehow. There were small shells along the shelves...shells that she had collected over the years and planned to turn into lovely jewellery for family and friends but had never quite got around to it. There were also plants that her mum had kept alive in her absence and loads of gardening books, some of which she'd had for 20 years.

She could wake up, swing open the shimmering voile curtains that ran the length of the windows, and look out onto one of the most fantastic beaches in the world. It had soft, golden sand and a blue ocean with cliffs creeping up the edges and disappearing into a cloudless sky.

Lisa could hear her sisters chatting away in the kitchen next door. Her mom, Georgina, was with them, delighted to have all her girls back home.

Lisa's return last night meant there was now a packed house at Sunshine Cottage. Georgina screamed with joy when they returned from the airport. 'This is the happiest I've been for years," she said when they all piled through the door. Ever since she'd retired from her job as a junior school teacher, she'd been much more involved with the girls' lives and keen to help them when things went wrong.

Lisa wrapped her baby-blue bathrobe around her, feeling how much it enveloped her; she must have lost a lot more weight than she realised—the thing was huge on her, completely hanging off. She pulled the belt tightly and wandered into the kitchen.

"Coffee?" Her mum handed her a cup without waiting for the answer, ruffling her hair as Lisa went over to join her sisters. Sophia had already left for work at Topaz, the up-market, crazily-expensive clothes shop in Cove Bay where she'd worked for the past couple of years. It suited Soph down to the ground, but, frankly, Lisa didn't know how she did it—being inside all day, dealing with the whims and fancies of rich, old women who had more money than sense.

Can you imagine a day spent discussing pearl over gold buttons and how to accessorise a £1,000 dress? Lisa couldn't. She hated to be inside. She was much happier in the fresh air, surrounded by nature.

"Why's Soph gone in so early?" she asked.

"She's preparing for a fashion show they're having in the shop. We're all going to it."

"OK, that sounds exactly like the sort of thing I want to do on an evening," said Lisa sarcastically.

"Come on - we're all going to support her. You'll love it when you get there - especially when you see the models she's got."

"Yeah, I'm sure," said Lisa. "Are you two not working today?" Isabella and Emma were both in bathrobes, and didn't look like they were heading anywhere soon.

"I start at 11:30 a.m.," said Emma. "That's when the bar opens. You should come down and see it there now. The place has been transformed since the Salcombe Sharks came to town. It's THE place to be."

"Who are the 'sharks'?"

"They're a rugby team. They are really good, and they're great fun. Everyone's been going down to watch them train. Their first match is coming up. It's going to be awesome."

"Not sure about rugby," said Lisa. That was an understatement. She couldn't think of a more pointless way to spend the day.

"You don't have to be a rugby fan to enjoy the social side of it. The players are great fun, and they have lots of functions there, organised by yours truly."

"You organise the football games?"

"No, I don't organise football games because they're not a football team. It's rugby. Aren't you listening?"

"Yes, sorry - rugby. Of course. Well, that makes all the difference. How long have you been doing that?"

"Did you read none of my emails?" asked Emma, hands on hips and a mock admonishing tone to her voice. "I've been there since they arrived. People travel to see them from all over Devon. It's brilliant. The bar has TV screens showing all the latest sports and good food. Hundreds of hunky men are there, and the bar manager's gorgeous."

"Who's the bar manager?"

"Me," said Emma. "No, you didn't read any of my emails. I wasted my time."

"Sorry, I did read them," Lisa replied. "I thought you worked in the bar, but you're clearly much more important than that. Sorry, Emms, I get a bit confused about sport."

"Matt - the guy you were on the plane with - he's the team's manager, and he used to play rugby for Scotland. He's lovely. He's like our big brother. He's here all the time eating mum's cakes."

"Yeah, he's always here because he lives in a horrible, dingy flat," said Isabella. "It's right between my hair salon and Soph's shop. I think he's desperate to get out of there."

"Oh, I always thought he was here all the time because he's taken a fancy to one of your girls. I'd been hoping one of you would end up dating him. He's such a nice guy," said their mother, looking from daughter to daughter.

"Really?" said Lisa. "He didn't seem all that special when I met him, just this angry sports nut who kept bashing into me."

"Oh, he's lovely. Lovely," said her mum. "He's a real gentleman. I don't know why you're all single with so many handsome sportsmen in town. You should see them, Lisa; they're a handsome bunch."

"I'm not remotely interested in men," said Lisa, with a shudder.

"No, I imagine you just want to go out and have fun and not even think of settling down just yet, after what that horrible man did," said Isabella.

"I still can't believe Peter behaved like that. He's the worst person ever. You don't mind us talking about it, do you? I'm sure you've forgotten all about him while you've been away, but he annoys me whenever I see his stupid, smug face. I want to punch him," said Emma.

"Have you seen much of him?" asked Lisa.

She tried to sound casual, as if it was a general enquiry off the top of her head and not something she had been thinking about endlessly.

"We see him around and about, you know. We tend to ignore him," said mom. "Your father told him if he came anywhere near the house, he'd hit him with a shovel."

"I spoke to him once," said Isabella. "He came into the hairdressing salon, and I refused to cut his hair. It caused quite a stir."

"Why would he go to a ladies' hairdressing salon?" asked Emma. "There's an excellent barber shop in Salcombe."

"Oh, you know what he's like. He's very fancy, isn't he? He has to have the best of everything."

Lisa could imagine that. Peter was preened to perfection and immaculate at all times.

"And I suppose he also wanted to find out about Lise and what she was up to," added Isabella.

"Why do you say that? Does he ever mention me?" asked Lisa.

There was silence.

"You might as well tell her," said her mum. "She's going to find out."

Lisa looked at her mom and her sisters.

"Find out what? What's happened? He's getting married, isn't he? I knew it."

"He said he wants you back."

"What?"

"He's finished with the dancer. He misses you."

"I can't believe this," said Lisa, shaking her head and standing up from the table. "I assumed that the two of them were living together by now. I haven't heard anything from him since I went to Edinburgh."

"No, well, we made him promise, absolutely promise, not to contact you while you were away. We told him he had to give you a break...give you time to get your head straight. We told him that he owed you that, at least."

"Does he know I'm back?" asked Lisa.

"No, sweetheart, he doesn't," said mum.

"Good," said Lisa, folding her arms across her chest. She felt anger and upset welling inside her. She knew she ought to feel satisfaction and pleasure that it had all gone wrong for him, and now he wanted her back. But she didn't feel like that...she felt bereft. He'd wrecked everything, caused her complete and utter heartache, and for what? For nothing. For a short fling that had ended with him wanting Lisa back. It was utter lunacy. She felt as if she'd been punched in the stomach. Why the hell couldn't he go away? Just disappear and get out of her head and out of her heart.

LISA WALKED INTO HER BEDROOM; she needed to be alone. She looked over the white sand to the sea, watching the waves crash on the beach and how the water thinned out as it rolled up the sand until just a few little bubbles remained. 'Angel foam,' they used to call it when she was younger. She needed to get outside and clear her mind.

TEN MINUTES LATER, Lisa was dressed and striding along the beach, swinging her arms by her side as she went. She'd planned to go for a gentle stroll in the fresh air when she set off, but it was turning into a power walk. She was so filled with anger and confusion she was taking it out on the sand and the sea air; her fists were balled up, her feet stomped, and her teeth were clamped together. It was all she could do to stop herself from crying. She'd been back here for less than a day and already freaking Peter was in her head and filling her with rage and confusion. How dare he make her feel like this?

Everything seemed to be going so well. She was starting to forget about him. Now, this. His reckless dalliance with the slutty dancer was over. He wanted her back. Well, he could forget that. She would no more go back to that clown than stick her head in the oven.

"Whoa…slow down."

Lisa spun around angrily to see Matt standing there.

"Why such a rush? I went to your house, and your mom said you'd gone for a walk on the beach. I didn't know you were going for some world record."

"I'm not feeling very talkative," said Lisa, continuing her fast pace. "I feel like punching someone, not talking to them."

"I'm pretty tough," said Matt. "Feel free to punch me."

Lisa felt tears pricking in her eyes. This was the last thing she wanted. She shouldn't be crying another tear over that horrible man.

She folded her arms and turned away, carrying on her speed walk along the beach.

"Hey, Lisa. Come on. Stop. What on earth's the problem?"

"Please, just leave me alone," she said, as tears escaped and began running down her cheeks. "I need some time to think."

"Come and sit down," said Matt, directing her to the rocks in front of them. "Here, come on. Sit down and tell me what's wrong."

Lisa perched on the edge of the rock and dropped her head into her hands. She felt so weak with anger and frustration. She couldn't bring herself to speak.

"It might help to talk about it."

She sat in silence, trying to form the words to explain how she felt. She was surprised by how quiet Matt was; he didn't pressure her to speak or push her to talk to him. He sat there. It was comforting, just being there, not feeling the need to speak, but also not being alone.

AFTER A FEW MINUTES of silence in which she composed herself and stopped crying, she looked up at Matt. He was looking patiently down at her.

"I was going out with this guy. He was my fiancé. His name was Peter, and I loved him. I thought about him all the time. I imagined we'd be together forever. I never considered my life without him in it. In my head, I had the house, the family, the life all planned. He was everything."

Matt leaned over and put his hands on hers. He didn't say anything. He just waited. It warmed her to see that someone who had appeared so brutish and masculine was being so tender and kind.

"He broke my heart."

Matt squeezed her hands and shifted closer to her on the rocks. "Had you known him long?"

"I met him about three years ago," Lisa said. "I was twenty-one and working in the gardens of Suffolk Manor. Do you know it? The big house on the road that runs past Salcombe? It has stunning gardens."

"Yes, I know it well."

"I loved working there. I'm obsessed with gardening. Then when this handsome guy called Peter Morgan started there, it seemed perfect. He seemed perfect. My life fell into place."

Lisa dropped her head into her hands again and started crying. She couldn't help herself. Just the thought of those early days and the great love they'd felt for one another...it had all seemed wonderful. How the hell could it have ended up like this?

"I don't want to talk about it," she said.

Lisa sat in silence, thoughts of Peter whirring through her mind.

"What do you love about gardening," asked Matt, realising that she wasn't ready to talk about Peter yet. Lisa took a deep breath and smiled.

"Everything," she replied. "I like taking a patch of earth that's unremarkable and plain and turning it into a wondrous extravaganza of colour and perfume."

"That certainly sounds good," said Matt.

"Flowers have everything. I've never been much of a sports fan like you, but with flowers...well, with any gardening, it brings all the senses to life. You see the ground transform as you work. You can smell it, feel it. Do you know? The whole area around you changes and becomes lovelier, and it's all because of what you're doing. I adore that."

Lisa looked up shyly, but Matt just nodded and smiled. He loved how her warm and open face came to life when she talked about her passion for gardening. It reminded him of his love for rugby. However, he couldn't ever remember talking about it as lyrically as she was talking about her love of flowers. There was something captivating about her; she was so ethereal, so honest and vulnerable. He leaned in more closely; he could smell a warm, pine scent in her hair.

"Tell me more," he said.

"You'll have to shut me up if I get too boring."

"I will," said Matt.

She explained that the thing she loved more than anything with gardening was that nothing happened quickly. Life today moved rapidly; newness was what everyone craved—the latest handbag

NOW, the latest lipstick NOW, car NOW. But flowers wouldn't be rushed. They took their time, did their thing, and demanded your attention. The rules were pretty simple and yet not simple at all. Some plants needed shade, others sunshine; some plants needed lots of watering, but others could be overwatered with a drop too much.

"You know what else I like about gardening," she added.

"Go on…"

"I like that flowers and plants show the coming of the seasons. I know that probably sounds naff to you, but I have always loved seeing flowers bloom as they herald the arrival of spring. I just love that moment when winter is swept away by the soft first brush of spring,"

"You talk so romantically about it all," said Matt.

"I know you think I'm daft; everyone does. I don't care. I love flowers, and I love walking in sun-dappled parks. I love trees too - they have such different looks and personalities - little individuals with quirks and needs, just like humans. Unlike humans, they don't turn on you at a moment's notice and run off with a glamorous ballerina, then regret it all and come running back just when you're getting yourself together."

"Ha," said Matt. "Why don't you tell me about this dork." She seemed calmer now…more relaxed.

"I've called him a few names over the past few months, but I'm not sure that 'dork' has been one of them."

"I'm happy to think of a few more names if you want," he said. "Tell me how you met him."

"As I said, I was doing this gardening job, and Matt had just finished his degree at Bristol Uni. He's very bright, much more intelligent than me. His parents had moved to the area, so he came back after graduating and was just looking to make money over the summer before returning to the uni to study law. So, we ended up working in the same place.

"He loved chopping trees down, and he preferred to dig the land in the fields on the edge of the estate to tending to the flowers up near the big house, so I didn't see him all day, every day, but we'd catch up in our breaks. I'd get so excited about the 20-minute drink breaks because he was always so sweet to me...so bright, funny and warm. He was immaculately well-dressed all the time...even when doing the gardens, which amused me. And he'd make a bee-line for me. To be honest, I couldn't believe he liked me. I mean, he was this handsome man who the girls working there that summer loved. I'd hear them talking about him and his smartly-pressed shirts and perfect hair, but for some reason, he liked me."

Matt bit his tongue. What was this woman talking about? She was lovely: fresh and natural. It was no wonder the guy liked her. Lisa was different from the other women he knew. She was the polar opposite of the over-pampered and preened PR and corporate women he was used to seeing. Those women looked great, but they weren't beautiful like Lisa. Their faces didn't transform when they spoke about their passions; their emotions weren't written all over their faces for everyone to see. Their gym-honed bodies looked great with fake tans, but they weren't soft and vulnerable like Lisa. The woman was beautiful; her hair fell naturally, not tied up with bows and pins, not full of colour and sprays.

Lisa had no idea what thoughts were running through Matt's mind, and she wasn't knocking herself when she expressed surprise about Peter's interest in her. She wasn't unattractive, but she knew she was pretty plain. She always thought of herself as having a simple, straightforward, forgettable face. Everyone told her she had nice hair; it was long, thick and dark, but she hadn't a clue what to do with it; it just hung there. When Isabella got hold of her, she would transform Lisa's hair, but Lisa wasn't very good at doing it herself - she just didn't have the skills or the inclination to battle with tongs and hairspray.

Peter hadn't seemed to mind this at all. He seemed to like her, and though there were younger, prettier girls working there that summer, he didn't look at them; he just chatted to Lisa.

Their boss, Nancy Havers, was aware of the growing closeness between her employees and bought them theatre tickets to watch plays in town and allowed them to sneak off early so they could spend more time alone. "You just make sure you don't get hurt," she said pointedly, and Lisa promised she wouldn't. How odd that statement seemed now, given everything that had happened since. Lisa knew she would have to go visit Nancy soon and see whether she could get her old job back. She must remember to mention that comment. Did Nancy always suspect something was going on?

Lisa felt a tear roll down the side of her face. She moved to wipe it away, but Matt got there first; in a tender gesture, he stroked a finger across her face, taking the tear with it.

She stopped and looked down. "Carry on," he said gently.

"Well, it continued like that; me working for Nancy, who gave me more responsibility in the gardens. She made me head gardener, which I know sounds a bit odd, and it sounds like it should be a role done by an old man with a pipe and overalls, but it was a position with quite a lot of responsibility. I had twelve gardeners working for me, and though Peter would eventually mock me for being a gardener while he was a qualified lawyer, I was making a pretty good wage. Most importantly: I loved it, and I was good at it.

"Nancy sent me on a leadership training course. I was doing well until it all fell apart with Peter, and I disappeared and ran away."

"You could easily go back there," said Matt. "She clearly thought a lot of you."

"Yes, I will. I'll talk to her, but Sophia said she's selling the house. She's quite old, and it's all too much for her. I don't suppose she'd want me there if it's going through a sale."

"Worth a try?" asked Matt, seeing how much her job had meant to her. "I think it would be worth popping in to see her. Even if she's selling it, it could be months or years before it all goes through, and whoever buys it will need staff there."

"Yes, I will. I owe her an explanation in any case. I'll go and see her later in the week."

"Do you want to get a coffee?" Matt asked. "I'm chilly; I don't know about you?"

As soon as he said it, Lisa realised she was really cold. It was a beautiful day; she had felt warm earlier when she'd been striding full-speed along the sun-dappled beach, but sitting still had left her feeling chilly.

"Coffee would be great," she said. Matt moved his hands off hers, and it was strange; as soon as he moved them, she felt an emptiness creep all over them. It had been nice to be touched again, even if only by a kind stranger. She looked up, and Matt had his hand to help her. She'd been wrong about him. He was a kind and thoughtful man, and she could see why her sisters were so fond of him.

WITH A FROTHY CAPPUCCINO in front of her, she looked up at Matt.

"Tell me a little bit about this rugby thing then. I don't know anything about it. How does it all work? And what are you doing basing yourselves here? Anyone can see that it's gorgeous, heavenly and wonderful in Cove Bay, but I'd be lying if I said it had been a magnet for leading sports teams over the years."

"Ha! Well, we're based at the old Salcombe Rugby Club. I live in Cove Bay, next to your sister's salon, but I spend all my time at your house because your mum makes the best cakes on the planet.

"I guess rugby for me is like gardening is to you. It's been in my life for as long as I can remember. I used to play rugby when I was a little kid and was a pretty decent outside centre when I was older. I was in the Scotland team and did well. Do you know the names of many rugby players?"

"No," said Lisa, with a raise of her eyebrows. She certainly didn't know the names of 'many'. To be honest, she'd struggle to think of the name of one.

"OK. Not to worry. Well - I was a decent player in my day, but age and injuries caught up with me, and I decided to retire. I didn't want to let go of the sport I'd made my name in, though...I wanted to give kids the opportunities I had as a youngster. I wanted to get involved with a club that allowed me to bring in great players, build a great team and, alongside that, set up a youth academy and junior sides. I wanted the best coaches, the best facilities, and I wanted to do it all where it hadn't been done before, you know - not in a big city with an established reputation, but somewhere smaller. Like Salcombe. I wanted to introduce new fans to the game."

"That's great. How's it going so far?"

"It's been a long haul. As soon as I was approached by the Exeter management and told that the club would be moving, I knew I wanted to be involved. It took us a while to get the planning permission to build a bigger stadium, but the place is amazing now. We had to ensure decent roads to the stadium and that nothing would disturb residents. I've had quite a few battles...you must have heard of them, people out demonstrating, trying to stop us from coming. I don't think they understood the ethos - we wanted to invest in a town's kids and use sport for the good of an area, but people were campaigning to keep us out!"

"Really? I don't remember that at all."

"The application was in the business's name, Falcon Trading. There were petitions and marches and everything."

"Oh, Yes, I do remember," said Lisa, suddenly recalling the banners and parades through the streets. "Oh, God. Yes, I remember that clearly. But I didn't pay much notice. I didn't realise it was for a rugby team. I just thought it was a new office block they were objecting to."

"They were objecting to everything," Matt said. "I could do no right for months. It's been a long, hard road. I retired five years ago and have been trying to sort all this out since Exeter called and told me that the club needed to move. But it's OK now. We have a thriving club full of decent players."

"How do you get the money to buy decent players when you're just starting out? And where do you get them from?"

"The money comes from investors, sponsors and advertisers. I spend a lot of time encouraging companies to get involved with us. We've done well, to be fair, and have pulled in some big names. Apple are one of the main sponsors, so we're OK for cash and computers.

'When it comes to recruitment, I've got a network of scouts looking out for talented players, and I know many of the upcoming stars myself. We got the go-ahead to move in at the beginning of this year. The first game is this Saturday; we're desperate for a good turnout…and a good victory. Fingers crossed."

Lisa crossed her fingers and held them up in front of her face.

"Now back to you, Ms Lopez. I want to know more. Where had we got to out there?" Matt asked, indicating the rocks visible to the side through the glass in front of the cafe.

"First, tell me about Peter, then tell me what happened between the two of you."

"Peter, blimey. Well, in short, I fell in love with him. We are very different people, but that didn't seem to matter. He was ambitious; he wanted to be the best lawyer ever. I wanted to create a nice life for myself, and Peter was at the centre of that life."

"And what happened?"

"Things between us changed when he finished his legal training and became a fully-fledged lawyer. He was doing something very different, and I was still doing the same thing in the same place. I sometimes became jealous when I heard about the new girls he was mixing with at his fancy lawyer's office; they sounded so together and sophisticated. It was like he had this other life…with them. I'd come home with dirt on my hands, clutching bunches of wildflowers, and he'd be there in his designer suits, having been to some fancy restaurant. I wasn't jealous; I've never wanted a corporate life. I felt he was living a different life from me, which was a little unnerving at times.

"He became a bit nasty about it if I'm honest. He'd tell me how lovely all the women in his office were and made me feel like I was a second-class citizen. He said I'd feel frumpy and dowdy if I ever came to his office, so I kept away. I didn't go to any of his work functions or meet him for lunch or anything. I felt I was too shabby and poorly dressed to go there.

"Then it got a bit more personal, and he told me I needed to lose weight and dress better. He made me feel awful, but at the time, I thought he was doing it to help me, so I could learn from this new life he was living."

"He sounds like a prize pillock," says Matt. "I mean, he's only working as a trainee solicitor at a little law firm in Salcombe; he's not the bloody Attorney General, is he? How many times did he advise the UK government on Brexit?"

"The way he talked about his job, you'd think he was advising all the governments in the world. The other thing he did was text people constantly. He'd always be sending messages, and when I asked who he was writing to, he'd say: 'Just a work thing.' He'd never say 'John in the office, or 'Margaret, a client.' It was always an unspecified and unexplained 'work thing,' I began to think it was odd that he was texting work colleagues in the evenings and at weekends. Wouldn't you email work-related information from the office in a more formal way?'

Matt had his eyebrows raised as he looked at me.

"I know what you're thinking: I must be insane, but it was a gradual process of me feeling less and less worthy, and it's only now, afterwards, that I can see how awful it all was."

"Actually, I wasn't thinking that you must be insane," said Matt with a gentle smile. "I thought that he must be. How could any man behave like that?"

"I don't know," said Lisa. "I don't know why he became so horrible. All I know is that in December, everything fell apart. I love Christmas, so I made great plans to have the best Christmas ever with Peter. I thought he might finally sit down with me and set a date. We'd been engaged for a year, and everyone wondered why we weren't planning the wedding. I thought that if we had the most amazing Christmas ever, it would help make him realise how wonderful I am. Ha! I'm such a dork." She smiled at Matt as she used his word. "I think I could get to like that word."

"It's a good word," he agreed.

Lisa explained how she'd cut down the most enormous Christmas tree she could find and dragged it through the forest back to the car; she decorated it and prepared Peter's favourite food - steak and chips. The table was set, and the food was all on the side, waiting to be cooked. She glanced at the clock - he was late. She sent a text, no reply. She called his mobile, no response.

Thinking back, she couldn't remember what it was that had motivated her to get in the car and drive to his office. Lots of people are late getting home from work. Why didn't she just wait? There must have been something else in her head warning her, telling her to drive up to the office as she had never done before and find out what was going on for herself.

She walked into the unfamiliar reception, straight past the receptionist (who was not all glamorous and lovely, as Peter had described her, but rather plain). She walked into Peter's office, and there he was, pants around his ankles, a dress thrown across the desk, and a lot of grunting and sighing. It was like a scene from a movie. She felt almost detached from it as it played out in all its technicolour glory in front of her.

"Shit, I'm sorry," said Matt, putting his big hands on top of Lisa's, as he had at the beach. "What a fucking idiot."

"The worse thing was, he didn't seem bothered that I'd caught him. I know he must have been, but his pride prevented him from showing any sort of remorse. He just looked up and seemed surprised to see me, as if I'd turned up when he was sitting at his desk, going through his paperwork. As if this was, really, all my fault."

Lisa remembered how she had stood there, rooted to the spot, staring for what felt like hours. It had probably only been seconds, but it had felt like the longest time. Then she'd rushed out, running as fast as she could. She didn't hear him calling her back; she didn't hear the receptionist ask if she was OK. She just ran for her car and drove like a maniac until she was back at her mum and dad's house. She let herself in, flung the door behind her and collapsed onto her bed, a mess of sadness and misery.

Her whole life had been geared around Peter, and her plans were woven around the two of them spending their lives together. Now it was all over.

Her dreams for their future had been smashed to pieces in front of her...there was no way their relationship could survive this.

"What did you do?" asked Matt.

The truth was that she hadn't known what to do...she'd had no idea how to move forward. Her life had been on hold for the past year, waiting for this man to finalise their wedding plans so they could begin their fantastic life together as man and wife. It wasn't supposed to have ended up with him on the desk, half-naked and panting, and her standing there in front of him, her hands still raw from dragging a Christmas tree home all alone; her mind still filled with plans to make this Christmas better than any Christmas before it. Nothing made sense.

"I remember being on my bed at mum and dad's and pulling the duvet over my head as I sobbed uncontrollably, howling in the dark like a wounded animal. Then I heard a gentle knocking on the door.

'Lisa, it's Sophia. Please open the door.'"

Lisa described how she had dragged herself out of the nest she'd created and opened the door to Sophia.

"What's the matter?" she asked as Lisa sat back on her bed.

"It's Peter," Lisa said. "He's having an affair with a woman at work."

Sophia sat down next to her and talked for hours until darkness descended on their pretty yellow beach house, and the rest of the family could be heard coming in from work and speaking in guarded whispers in the kitchen. Every few minutes, one of them would knock on Lisa's door to check she was OK; she'd relay the story's details and listen as they'd gasp in horror at what Peter had done. Soon they were all sitting on Lisa's bed, sharing their anger and disappointment as she alternated between sobbing and shrieking in rage. "I don't know why he did this. Why would he do this?" she moaned while her sisters shook their heads supportively and comforted her in her sadness.

In the middle of all the hurt and tears, Lisa heard a knock on the front door and knew it would be Peter. It hurt her that he'd taken so long to come. 'Let him in,' she said to her sisters, and soon Peter stood in the doorway of her bedroom, no longer dishevelled, but all dressed up and looking smart.

"She misunderstood," he said, smiling appealingly at Emma. "It's not how she thought it was."

"What? You having sex with another woman on your desk wasn't what she thought it was? What was it then?"

"It was a business meeting," he said, but even he appeared to recognise how ridiculous that must sound, as his usual confident demeanour dissolved, and he shuffled his feet and lowered his gaze. "Look, can I just talk to Lisa on my own?"

Lisa looked at him and her sisters, who glared at her fiancé with undisguised fury. Something about Peter's manner, the way he had gone home and tidied himself up before coming over, annoyed her. It was as if she were the last thing on his mind...preserving his public image was much more important to him.

"I don't want to talk to you right now," she said, even though she did. She wanted to talk to him with every fibre of her being. She wanted him to beg her forgiveness, take her in his arms, and promise that nothing like that would ever happen again. But she looked at him, shuffling his feet and oozing impatience, and decided to put herself first for the first time ever.

"No," she said.

He looked up. He'd expected to be able to walk all over her and win her back straight away. "Come on, Lisa. This is ridiculous. We have to talk about it."

"She said 'no'," said Emma, standing up and gently pushing him out the door.

"I HAVEN'T SEEN HIM SINCE," said Lisa, looking at Matt. "I left for Edinburgh to stay with my friend Charlie for a couple of weeks and ended up staying for months. I had lots of calls and messages, of course. Every day I had missed calls from him until around two weeks ago when all the communication stopped, and I assumed that he and the naked on the desk woman had moved in together or were getting married or something. It turns out that he stopped all contact because my sisters warned him not to contact me while I was in Scotland. They warned him to leave me alone. So I never got to hear his latest news."

"His latest news?"

"That he had finished with the woman he was having an affair with and wanted me back."

"Blimey," said Matt. "He wrecked everything for a fling?"

"Yep."

"That's rubbish."

"Yep."

"Fancy another coffee?"

"Sure," said Lisa. "But I'll get this one." She was aware that he didn't have much money. The way Isabella had described his flat, right next to her salon, sounded awful.

"No, you won't," replied Matt, signalling to the waiter.

"What made you choose Edinburgh as a place to go to?" he asked. "Seems a strange place for you to disappear to."

"You mean because I'm a country bumpkin?"

"Well - you admit that you like the countryside and the seaside, and many places are closer than Edinburgh. So many places in England that you could have headed for."

"I went there because my friend Charlie lives there. She's a super-cool and trendy Edinburgh type these days, but she used to live in Cove Bay. I talked to her after the Peter incident, and when she told me to come and stay awhile, I thought it made sense. She got me a job for six weeks at a stall in the flower market next to the beautiful castle. I healed while there and started to feel much better about life.

I came back feeling strong. But now I feel awful. It's like all that time I spent healing, and making myself better, has all been in vain. Hearing he's single and wants me back has thrown me. I don't know why..."

"Surely you don't want him back," said Matt. "You can't possibly want to share your life with someone who'd treat you like that."

"No, it's not that I want him back. It's just...I don't know. I never even thought I had the option to have him back before, so that had never occurred to me, and now I have, my head's all over the place."

"OK, repeat after me: I do not want that dork back in my life," said Matt. "Say it."

"I do not want that dork back in my life," she said.

"Louder," replied Matt.

"I do not want that dork back in my life."

People were looking now. Jen, the lady who runs the butcher's shop with her husband Willie, was peering over at them.

"People are staring at me."

Matt wasn't concerned.

"LOUDER," he instructed.

"I DO NOT WANT THAT DORK BACK IN MY LIFE," she shouted.

"Ha!" he said, high-fiving her. "Well done, girl. Now, I want you to come to our welcome drinks evening tomorrow night, OK? We will have a drinks-and-rugby get-together at the sports bar every Thursday after training. People can come down, meet the players and have a drink. I will come and find you if you're not there with your sisters. Understand?"

"Yes," she said meekly. "I understand."

CHAPTER 3

When Sophia came home from work, Lisa was waiting for her with a request that dazzled her. "Do you have any clothes I could borrow for the 'meet-the-players evening' tonight?" she asked.

Sophia dropped her handbag to the ground and hugged her sister. "It's a miracle," she said. "I never thought I'd see the day when you would want to get dressed up for something. Are you not well?"

"Ha, ha," said Lisa. "All my clothes are too big for me. I don't want to look like a clown in an oversized outfit."

"You will look like a princess when I finish with you. Come with me...."

Sophia's room was the exact opposite of Lisa's. Instead of a shelf lined with seashells she'd spotted on the beach and books about gardening, she had clothes, jewellery and shoes - my God, more shoes than you've ever seen in your life before.

"How many feet do you have?" asked Lisa, seeing shelf after shelf of pumps, sandals and boots in the en-suite bathroom that Sophia had transformed into a walk-in wardrobe.

"Do you want my help or not?" Sophia asked.

"Yes, please. I'll make no comments about you having so many pairs of shoes you could dress a centipede if you would please lend me a dress that will fit me."

Sophia disappeared into her wardrobe while Lisa sat down heavily on the bed.

"I went for a coffee with Matt," she said. She was unsure whether to share the news with her sisters, but if anyone could be trusted to keep a secret, it was Soph, who wasn't as 'teamy' as the others and tended to keep herself to herself, so she was unlikely to gossip. Not many people understood this about Sophia...she seemed to be always at the centre of everyone's attention because of her looks. She stood out simply by entering the room. But the truth was that she was a very private person and very discrete.

Sophia appeared out of the vast wardrobe, clutching a collection of dresses with her mouth open and her eyebrows raised.

"What? Like a date with Matt?" she said.

"No. No. Not a date at all. He was kind to me after all this nonsense with Peter, the dork."

"The dork? Good name."

"Thank you. It was Matt's description, but I think it's rather fitting."

"Me too. Do you think Matt likes you? It's odd to invite someone out for coffee like that when you don't know them well. Perhaps he thinks it was a date?"

"No, definitely not. He bumped into me yesterday when I was crying and upset, and he was being kind. That's all."

"You were crying? Why didn't you tell me something was wrong? Is everything OK now?"

"Yes, it was just that mom, Isabella and Emma told me about Peter saying he wanted me back. It kind of threw me. I went for a walk along the beach and got upset. I bumped into Matt. He was being kind."

There was a gentle tapping on Sophia's door. Lisa turned to her sister. "Don't mention the Matt thing, please. I don't want everyone talking about it. He was just being kind."

"OK," said Sophia, playfully winking at Lisa as she opened her bedroom door. "Your secret's safe with me."

Isabella was standing outside the door, clutching a bottle of wine and three glasses. "I heard there was a party going on. Who the hell chose not to invite me?"

"Come in," said Sophia. "You won't believe what Lisa has got me doing."

"Soph is finding me something to wear to this players' drinks thing tonight," said Lisa. "My clothes are all huge on me."

"Ooh, let me do your hair," said Isabella. "I want to put a bit of body into that luxurious mane...get it all curly and looking gorgeous."

"I don't know," replied Lisa. She didn't want to look like a Barbie doll at the party.

"There are some pretty nice guys there," said Isabella.

"It's true," agreed Sophia, holding dresses up against Lisa to work out which ones would look best.

"Oh, I love that sky blue on you," said Isabella. "That suits you."

"I'm not sure. I think we need something a bit more vibrant with that dramatic dark hair. Maybe emerald green or scarlet would work?'

"Yes, scarlet lady, to lure the men."

"Not sure I want a man just now, thanks. I just want some help with clothes that fit."

"OK," said Isabella. "I won't go on about the men, but pretty please, can I do your hair?"

"Only if you promise not to make me look stupid."

"Here," said Sophia, handing Lisa a sleek red dress. "I've got some fab wedges to match, or it would work with white trainers if you'd be more comfortable."

"White trainers go with everything, honey," said Isabella, pouring them a glass of wine each. "The best thing to come out of lockdown was people wearing trainers instead of high heels."

Lisa slipped the lovely dress on and looked at herself in the mirror. "Mmmm...I'm not sure it's me," she said.

"Holy hell, Lise you look gorgeous. You're a goddamn film star," said Isabella.

"I feel like a transvestite or something. I feel so ungainly in it. I never wear dresses. Are you sure I don't look completely ridiculous?"

"You look lovely," said Sophia.

"Not ridiculous at all," said Isabella. "Now, let me do your hair, and you'll look spectacular."

In a moment of weakness, Lisa let her older sister tease her hair into a cascade of waves and curls. She sat, looking into the mirror as she was transformed. Isabella and Sophia muttered their appreciation while Lisa looked critically at the stranger she was being moulded into. She could see that it looked good, but did it look like her? She wasn't sure.

"Right, I better get ready," said Sophia. "Leaving in thirty minutes, right?"

Lisa and Isabella left Sophia to dress. Lisa had been so excited about seeing Matt tonight, but now she felt nervous. She felt so over-dressed, so silly, in this fancy dress and shoes and with her hair all bouffant and ridiculous. She was going to a sports bar, not to collect an Oscar.

She entered her bedroom and looked out through the enormous windows at the back of her house, out onto the sea beyond. Carefully, she removed the dress, eager not to mark it or crease it, and hung it on a hanger; then, she found a plain white shirt and jeans. The clothes were big on her, but that made them comfortable; they'd do just fine. She tied her crazy hair into a ponytail. The curls were still there; her sisters would be happy with that, but the rest of the outfit had gone.

Lisa emerged cautiously from the room, peering around to see whether her sisters were ready yet. There was no sign of them, so she wandered into the kitchen and sat in her mom's big rocking chair overlooking the beach. It was the same view offered by her bedroom - lovely and comforting When she heard her sisters coming, she stood up and faced them.

"What on earth have you done?" asked Sophia. "You looked drop-dead gorgeous; now you look as if you're all set to spend the evening cleaning the kitchen."

"I'm sorry; I just didn't feel myself in that getup."

"Come on then," said Sophia, shaking her head at Isabella. "It was progress that you tried, and at least your hair looks fantastic. Let's go."

Lisa flicked her hair. "I can't remember the last time I was all curly."

BY THE TIME the women reached the bar, it was packed. Emma and Matt were both right; it was the place to be. Lisa looked around in amazement. The area that used to be an old golf club bar and had stood unused and unloved for years was buzzing. TVs on the walls showed highlights from the players' games while people drank and chatted. Music blared.

"Soph, Lise, Issy, come here."

Emma called them over and led them to a second bar cut off by a velvet rope. There was room to breathe and stools to sit on in there. It was just what they needed.

"Can I get you ladies a drink?" asked Matt, coming up beside them and kissing Lisa warmly on the cheek.

"Oy, where's my kiss?" asked Emma, now back behind the bar and preparing to serve. Matt leaned over and kissed her on both cheeks before turning to Sophia and Isabella.

"You girls look fantastic," he said, shouting to make himself heard above the noise of chatter and Bruce Springsteen's dulcet tones.

Lisa immediately wished she'd worn the dress. Isabella and Sophia were both dressed up. The room was filled with attractive women, all made up to the nines and wearing skimpy clothes. Were they all here to try and get their hands on one of these sportsmen? Were any of them after Matt? He was a good-looking guy and looked particularly handsome in his jacket tonight. She'd never seen him in anything other than jeans and a sweatshirt before. Perhaps he was going out with one of these girls?

"Hey, dreamer, what are you thinking about? You're miles away."

"Sorry. I was just thinking about how lively and exciting this place is now. I remember the old, run-down golf bar that was here. We used to come here when we were kids and play. You've done well."

"Why thank you," said Matt. "It's not all my work, of course. Your sister was very involved in the whole thing. She came up with many ideas for developing the club, and having a 'meet-the-players night' during the season was one of them. She is a little superstar, your sister."

Did he like Emma? She hoped not. But why did she care? She and Matt were just friends. They'd had a friendly chat and been for a nice walk on the beach; that was it.

She turned back to her sisters. Sophia was scanning the room, looking as alluring and gorgeous as ever. "Who do you fancy then?" Lisa asked.

"I couldn't possibly say...too much choice," Sophia replied with a smile.

"Come on, if you had to spend the night with one of them, which one would it be?" she shouted above the loud music.

Lisa could feel herself getting drunk. It was a nice feeling. She felt relaxed and happy, and every time she glanced over to where the players were hanging out, she caught sight of Matt, smiling at her. He always seemed to be looking over.

"Well, the best-looking guy is Joe; he looks like a film star," said Sophia.

"I knew it, I knew it. You two would be the best couple in the world," said Lisa. "You're both beautiful."

Lisa had been introduced to Joe Harris soon after they arrived. He had kissed her hand and been charming, but all the time seemed to be looking at Sophia, and Sophia, for her part, had started doing a lot of hair flicking and pouting.

He was the team's star player. He looked like a young and handsome Elvis Presley. He had a smoulder, a perfect body and millions of pounds worth of sponsorship deals. He played in the centre for the Sharks and England and made regular appearances in the tabloids. He'd been 'discovered' by Jonny Wilkinson and spent a lot of time with the World Cup star.

Lisa knew nothing about rugby, but she'd heard of Jonny Wilkinson, and she knew a divine specimen of masculinity when she saw one. He was beautiful in a conventional, Hollywood-heartthrob sort of way. He had a square jaw/stubble combo and the most beautiful green eyes Lisa had ever seen.

He and Sophia would be perfect together, with her milky blonde hair, always immaculately styled, her large blue eyes and delicate features, like Grace Kelly; she was the Barbie doll to his Ken. Lisa just needed to get them together.

"Why don't you talk to him?" asked Lisa. "You two would make the world's most perfect couple and have the most beautiful children ever."

"Ha! No thanks," said Sophia. "Can you imagine feeding that ego? Anyway, look at him; cheerleaders and hangers-on surround him. I don't need all that."

"Oh, they're cheerleaders. I didn't realise. I didn't know that rugby had cheerleaders."

"It doesn't usually, but one of their key sponsors is Apple, the tech company, and the bright sparks in the US who signed off the agreement insisted on cheerleaders, music at half time and all sorts of razzmatazz. It drives Matt nuts."

"Can't Matt just say he doesn't want it?" asked Lisa.

"To be fair, he does refuse most of it, and Steve Bence, the guy from Apple who Matt deals with, is brilliant, and he rejects most of the demands from California."

"But not the demand for cheerleaders?" said Lisa.

"No, I think they're stuck with them for the season's opening games, then Steve said they can phase them out."

"Are all these tanned women over there cheerleaders?"

"Yep, all the beautiful, painfully-skinny girls with massive boobs and tons of makeup are cheerleaders. If in doubt, look at their colour; if they are orange, they're on the cheer squad."

"These women have devoted their lives to jumping around and shaking pompoms," came a voice to the side of them. It was Maisie Clock, the woman who ran *Flip Flop Bar* in Cove Bay with her handsome husband, Will. "Think about that for a second, ladies. Jumping around with pompoms full-time."

"Some cheerleaders are very talented," said Lisa. "I'm not a fan of the burnished orange skin or the 20" of make-up, but they are pretty athletic."

"They annoy me," said Maisie.

"Me too," said Sophia. "You're too nice for your own good, Lisa."

'They don't bother me at all. Come on, Soph. You work in a shop, and I'm an unemployed gardener. Are we much better?"

"Hell, yes. I'm going to have a chain of fashion stores and a personal-stylist company and be fashion advisor to the President's wife, and you are going to be the best gardener in the world, with your range of books and a TV series. We'll be famous, rich and stylish. They will always be jumping up and down, waving pom-poms. There's a difference."

It was unusual for Sophia to be so bitchy.

"They seem harmless," said Lisa.

"They sleep with the players all the time. I'm not a fan, either," said Emma. "More drinks?"

Sophia reached over to pick up her empty glass and hugged Emma. "Thank you, lovely; a glass of wine would be perfect. Drinks for everyone else? Let's stop talking about the cheerleaders and get drunk."

Had Lisa touched a raw nerve or something? It seemed so.

"Have Emma or Isabella been out with any of the players?" she asked Sophia.

"Emma's very close to Will Burns. That guy there."

Lisa looked over to see Emma chatting to a rather ungainly, clumsy-looking guy who scratched his head, leaving his hair standing on end. He shuffled uncomfortably as she talked to him.

"Does she fancy him?"

"I don't know. You know what Emma's like: she throws men straight into the friend zone as soon as she meets them."

"Yes, very true. What about Izzy?"

"I think she likes Ted - over there, see."

Sophia indicated a big bear of a man standing in the corner. He looked solid and had his blonde hair cut into a short back and sides.

He had an aloofness to him as he stood there, with his shoulders back and his head held high as if he were on the parade ground.

"He's ex-military, in case you couldn't tell."

As Lisa looked over, Ted caught her eye, so she looked away quickly, and she saw Joe chatting with a couple of giggling cheerleaders. Oh, God, perhaps Soph was right? Maybe they were all sleeping around.

"Hello, beautifuls," said Matt, appearing between herself and Sophia. "Are you enjoying your first Sharks party?"

"I am," Lisa said. "I've been admiring the cheerleaders."

Sophia excused herself and headed for the bathroom while Lisa and Matt continued to chat.

"They are nice girls," said Matt. "People call them 'shark bait' and say they're only here to find a man, but I think they're a nice bunch."

Lisa just nodded.

"What are you up to tomorrow?" he asked, gesturing at Emma to provide everyone with more beer.

"Nothing, really," said Lisa. "I suppose I should go and see Nancy at some point to discuss getting my job back, but I haven't made any plans."

"Ahh, the job can wait," said Matt. "I think you should come to lunch with me tomorrow."

"Lunch?"

"Yep, and I'm not taking 'no' for an answer, so it would be much easier for all of us if you just said 'yes' straight away."

"OK, then 'yes'," she said meekly. "That would be nice."

He put his arm around her and kissed her on the cheek before ruffling her hair in its high ponytail. "You're all curly," he said. "Did you realise?" Then he winked at her and disappeared into the crowd.

She loved that he had no idea how much effort and time went into making hair curly. He thought it had just happened, and she might not even know about it.

CHAPTER 4

"*H*ow's your head?" Matt had come to pick her up at the house. "And what's going on with your hair? It's all straight again."

"I'm afraid there's not a very exciting explanation. I washed it and dried it straight," she explained. "And in answer to your first question - my head is terrible. I feel like I might die. I'm never drinking again. Life is very painful today."

"Ha, ha. Yes, I feel pretty much the same. Did you have a good night, though?"

"Oh yes, it was great. I really enjoyed myself. Honestly, I haven't had such a good night out in ages. The band was really good, and everyone was so friendly."

"I know. The band is great, isn't it? I'm glad you mentioned *Thermal Waves*. The lead singer is Jake Ellis's brother. Did you meet Jake? He's our captain."

"I think so," said Lisa, "but it's all a bit blurry now. I met so many handsome sportsmen that they're all starting to blend into one."

"I will have to stop inviting you there," said Matt. "Not sure I'm happy with you thinking they're all handsome. By the way, are your parents in? I should say hello."

"Yes, come in," said Lisa, showing him through to the kitchen and watching as he moved with ease between her parents, shaking her dad's hand and complimenting her mom.

"What's that?" he asked, standing confidently in the middle of the kitchen, pointing to an old, broken chest of drawers abandoned on the beach in front of them. Lisa had wondered that too. This was a small community and a tidy beachfront. It seemed astonishing that anyone would come and dump their garbage right outside her mum and dad's house.

"I've tried to move it, Matt, but it's a hell of a weight. I'll get the girls to come out and help me when they're in, but they're hard to pin down. Always out partying. You know what they're like."

"Indeed I do," said Matt. "I'll get some guys to come over and move it."

"No, there's no need to do that," said Dad. "I'll fix it."

"No, you won't. They'll be over this afternoon," said Matt assertively. "It can be part of their weight training."

"Thanks, son," her dad said. "Very kind of you."

They walked out to Matt's car, him on the phone to his coaches at the club, telling them to send players over to the beachfront to move the abandoned chest of drawers as soon as possible. He seemed to have enormous power at the club. She was glad that he was wielding it to help her parents.

"All sorted. It'll be done by the time we get back from lunch," he said, unlocking the car door for her and holding it open. "Now, sit back and relax. We're heading to a lovely little place I know in the Kingsbridge Estuary."

"Oh, that sounds lovely," said Lisa. She felt all warm and comfortable in his presence. He was a very calming and trustworthy sort of guy.

"Tell me - are you the team's coach or the manager?"

"I'm kind of the manager," he replied vaguely.

"What's the difference?" she asked.

"They both work on the playing side of the club. The coach is all about the players; the manager is all about the whole thing."

"I'd have thought that on the playing side of the club, the players are *the whole thing.*"

"Yes, you're right. I haven't explained that very well. So the coach works under my direction to create the best team on the pitch. As a manager, I also have responsibility for their fitness, travel, psychological preparation and everything that goes into making the players into winners on the pitch and off."

"OK," said Lisa. "I think I get it."

"Good," he replied. "And I'm very glad you enjoyed last night. How are you finding life back here after all that partying in Edinburgh? It must be strange to be home."

"It's great to be home," said Lisa. "I enjoyed Scotland, and as a place to go to forget, I could have chosen nowhere better. It was like another world. But my heart is here. Do you go to Edinburgh much?"

"Yes, a fair bit," said Matt. "I was born there and played for Scotland. I had been back there scouting for players at matches when we bumped into one another on the plane."

Lisa smiled. She knew about his Scottish connections. She'd read the notes in the team programme that Emma had brought home. He'd been a pretty good player in his day.

The familiar and beautiful landscape flew by as Matt drove along the coast road, heading towards their lunch venue. She told him about her trip north, from walking out of the bustling Edinburgh airport where so many people were congregating and circulating, hauling their bags around and catching up with loved ones. She had felt dazzled and horrified in equal measure.

Certainly, the size of the place had put her tiny problems into perspective, and though she could never live in a city centre, the relentlessness of it all had served to take her mind out of her problems. She began to gain some perspective and realise that, while she was sad, she would survive. It had been unpleasant, but she would recover and love again.

"There was this awful, tinny music playing as I walked out into the main foyer, and it suddenly seemed so silly, so out of keeping with the glamour of the place. Like the horrible music played on the phone while you're waiting to be connected at Isabella's hair salon. Not capital city music."

Matt smiled. "They probably want to keep everyone moving through the airport as quickly as possible. They play terrible music to hurry them along."

"You're probably right," she said. "I just wandered through it all, thinking how much Sophia would love it in the city, clip-clopping along the Royal Mile like a character from *Sex and the City*. It seemed strange that it was me there and not her."

"So, the Royal Mile was your favourite, was it?"

"I think George Street was my favourite place to wander. I loved it along there. And Princes Street, that was great too."

Lisa remembered it all so clearly, the arrival at the airport and the way she'd scanned the crowd looking for Charlie. That moment of relief when her great friend had rushed forward, waving her arms and squealing her delight. Then Lisa knew that she would be OK. She had made the right decision. Charlie wrapped her up in a big hug, holding her tightly as Lisa's strength deserted her, and she slowly collapsed, crying and bawling on her friend's shoulder as she explained what had happened. "What an absolute shit," Charlie had said. "Forget him. Stay here for a few months; have some fun."

"I was only going to stay for a couple of weeks," Lisa told Matt. "I hadn't planned anything or told anyone. I'd just jumped on the flight, but Charlie insisted. She said that she'd take care of everything.

"And she did," Lisa said to Matt. "She sorted me out, shook me down and made me feel a million times better."

Lisa thought back. It felt like it all happened years ago. They had left the airport and headed to Charlie's apartment, which was a riot of colours and artistry.

Charlie was an aspiring artist, and her brother Max was a fully-fledged professional artist with his own gallery and growing reputation.

"You painted all these?" Lisa had said, genuinely impressed with what she was looking at. "These are great."

"Thanks, lovely; Max thinks I'm too obsessed with yellow. I keep making everything a little bit yellower than it should be."

"Ha. Like my mum. Remember when she went on an art course years ago? She came home and painted the cottage yellow because it was the colour of creativity. Dad went nuts; he'd bought the cottage because it was an authentic old fisherman's cottage, and mum went and painted it the colour of sunflowers because she loved the artist Van Gogh at the time. She told us about a yellow house the artist shared with Gauguin, the French painter, in a city called Arles in Provence. She wanted our cottage to look just like it."

"I never knew that," said Charlie with a gigantic smile. "Now I love your mum even more. I assumed the cottage was yellow when your parents bought it. I didn't realise she'd painted it!"

"Yep, she painted it to look like Van Gogh's house. Well before I was born. The woman's well and truly bonkers."

Lisa's first evening in Edinburgh had been outstanding. They'd curled up on the sofa and demolished a bottle of wine while she ran through the story of what Peter had done, again and again. Charlie had let her talk, let her cry and let her punch the furniture.

When Lisa had finally calmed down and could talk properly, Charlie talked through all the fun things they could do while she was in Edinburgh. "Oh, and Max is around later," Charlie had said. "He's keen to catch up with you. He says he hasn't seen you for years."

Max had been off travelling the world so much, moving from India to Africa and enjoying a carefree life. Now, though, it appeared that he had settled down in Edinburgh.

"I can't wait to see him again. Oh, Charlie, I'm so glad I came here. This is just like the old days when you used to live near us in Cove Bay."

"It was lovely," Lisa said to Matt as they drove along. "I got on well with Max, and we became the three amigos, working from early morning until just after lunch. Charlie and I worked at the flower market, selling orchids, tulips and peonies in the shadow of the castle. the market was like heaven, with everything including fresh-cut flowers, exotic plants, pottery and ceramics, foliage, silk flowers and trees."

The first time Lisa saw the flower market, she couldn't believe it. She had worked in gardening all her life, but seeing this flash of colour and beauty in the middle of the city was something else. Many stalls had so many flowers they spilt out onto the pavement. It meant the whole area was a fiesta of colour.

"This is where you will be working," Charlie had said on Lisa's first day at work. She pointed to an incredibly gorgeous shop brimming with flowers. An old wooden sign hung outside, announcing, "Bundles of beautiful blooms." She had noticed the smell of sweet peas right away; their familiar scent had swirled around, catching her in its sickly embrace. "Wow, it's gorgeous," she had said to Charlie. "Just amazing."

Charlie had pointed to the shop across the road, where she worked. It was her own shop, and she was running it with Max, selling his art and a few of her paintings, along with some beautiful pottery from local artists. Max spent his days at his main gallery on Queen Street.

Lisa had been overjoyed when she saw the shop. After such a horrible period in her life, she was in this amazing city with these incredible friends, working in the most beautiful place she could imagine. It had been a huge tonic—exactly what she had needed. How could anyone think of broken hearts when there were flowers everywhere? She had loved that, in this most cosmopolitan of cities, there was this oasis of calm, this riot of colour, all created by like-minded people.

The car had stopped, and Matt was sitting there, listening to Lisa as she talked about the flowers and Waverley market. Lisa looked out the window. They were parked outside a beautiful little fish restaurant tucked away in the rocks. Matt switched off the engine and turned to look at her. They held each other's glance for what felt like ages until she looked away, embarrassed. He was really nice. She liked him a lot.

CHAPTER 5

*M*att strolled around the edge of the field, barking instructions. It was game day. This was a new team in a new area and getting off to a winning start was vital. The club had managed to get finance relatively easily, thanks to Matt's hard work, but if they were to keep getting financed and keep the crowds coming and the advertisers and sponsors rolling in, they needed to win. They had to be seen as a success story...a team that people wanted to be a part of.

They had to win today against Harlequins, a big London club that Matt had played for at the beginning of his career. Matt needed to show everyone in the local area that this was a winning side; a side worth supporting. But there were other reasons as well. Matt was keenly aware that Lisa was coming to watch the game and he wanted her to see him as a great success. Her ex had been some hot-shot lawyer. He had to show her that he was a successful guy too.

He smiled as he thought about her, this lovely, sweet woman who seemed to be carrying the weight of the world on her shoulders. He'd liked her since he first saw her on the plane—all trembly and nervous, tucking herself close to the window, trying not to make eye contact with anyone, just wanting to read her book.

He knew he hadn't made a good impression. He had such problems flying; he hated it, and his fear of aeroplanes made him angry and frustrated.

But, somehow, they'd got through that. They were good friends now; he liked spending time with her and being around her. He wanted to make her feel better. He knew she was making him feel better. There was something about her...something so natural. He had to take it slowly, though. If he went storming in there and did what he really wanted to do, he'd terrify her.

Also, he couldn't tell her the truth about himself. Not yet.

LISA WAITED for Charlie to answer the phone, smiling as she heard her friend's voice.

"I miss you so much," she said.

"I miss you too," replied Charlie, practically talking over her friend as they played verbal cat-and-mouse to share their news and enquire about each other's well-being.

"And have you bumped into Peter?"

"No, thank God. But get this...he's not with the dancer anymore. They have finished dating. It's all over, and he regrets what he did."

Her comment was greeted by silence from the other end.

"Charlie, are you still there?"

"Yes, I'm still here, but honey...promise me you aren't going to go back with him. Please..."

"No, no, no, of course, I'm not. I've got a new friend in any case. We're not dating or anything; we just enjoy spending time together. He's helping me to get over Peter. He's lovely."

"Oh. My. Freaking. God!" shrieked Charlie. "You so are dating. I can hear it in your voice. What's he like? Is he a billionaire?"

Lisa began to run through Matt's qualities, keeping her voice down, so her sisters didn't hear her. "He's lovely but - no - not a billionaire. He's a coach of the team and earns hardly anything and lives in a grotty flat, but he's really good fun. I'm going to watch the game this afternoon, then we've all been invited to a party when it's over. Honestly, this rugby team coming to the area has transformed our social lives. Even Mum and Dad are coming to watch the game. Emma's working in the club - managing the bar and helping with social events. Sophia comes out with us and sometimes isn't dressed head-to-toe in Chanel. It's flipping amazing."

"I'm so glad you're having such a great time," said Charlie. "You're making me want to come back to see what's going on."

"You must," said Lisa. "I'd love that. Bring Max. We should introduce him to my sisters; it's about time he met someone lovely."

"Your sisters aren't still single, are they? It's ridiculous...such a gorgeous group of girls. I can't believe Sophia doesn't have all these rugby players following her around, morning, noon and night."

"Oh, she does. There's a player called Joe; he's the world's most beautiful man, and he's clearly crazy about her, but she's not interested. She thinks they're all up to no good and are sleeping with the cheerleaders and fans. He'll have a bit of convincing to do if he wants to go out with her."

"Oh, I love it. I'll have to fly down and see you all. I've got a customer, so I can't talk now, but save one of those hunky guys for me. Now you have a great time at the game. Go get yourself all dressed up and knock 'em dead."

LISA HAD no plans to get "all dressed up" for the game. She planned to keep it light and casual and to be as comfortable as possible: jeans, a jumper and a warm jacket. She brushed her hair and decided to leave it down. She put Vaseline on her lips and was good to go. They were all going to the game except for Sophia, who had zero interest in sports. She loved the parties, but the prospect of sitting there, watching people throw the ball around and tackle one another. Nope. Wasn't going to happen.

Lisa felt the same if the truth be told, but she wanted to be there to support Matt. Their lunch date had been lovely, and he'd been so kind and generous. He hadn't pushed her at all. She felt comfortable with him. And if he did try to kiss her one day soon...well, that might be OK.

"Come on then," said her dad, as he piled them into the back of his car like they were all eight again. Living back at home reminded Lisa of being a child, not in a bad way; it was great to live with your own family as an adult, but it was odd considering she'd moved out and moved in with Peter a year ago. And now she was back and living in the room where she'd grown up.

Lisa could feel the excitement in the air as they walked to their seats in the stadium, they were great seats, right in front, near the coaching bench. She could see Matt striding purposefully around the edge of the grass, hands behind his back as he plodded. She felt a gentle tingle run through her as she watched him.

The atmosphere in the stadium was like nothing she'd experienced before. Her idea of an enjoyable time was working quietly and contentedly in the gardens. She'd never been in an atmosphere quite like this, where there was such sharing of passion. You could feel it buzzing in the air and on the faces of the young and old who'd gathered in this once-dilapidated stadium, now transformed by the sport.

Watching the game was a wonderful experience. The only problem was that she didn't have a clue what was going on. It was all much more complicated than she was expecting it to be. Lisa was surprised by how little she knew but how much she suddenly wanted to know. She would make it her mission to find out. For now, though, she looked for the players she knew. She could see Ted on second base, and she glanced at Isabella instinctively, but her sister seemed more interested in the hot dog she was eating than any potential romance with the man on the base. She could see Will, too, but no sign of Joe.

"Why isn't Joe playing?" she asked Emma.

"He's injured. Apparently, he broke his fingers in training."

"Ow, painful."

"Yes, he was trying to use his injury to convince Sophia to go out on a date with him, but she's not at all interested."

"I didn't realize he'd asked her out."

"What? Yes. He calls her every damn day. He says he's going to call her every day until she agrees to go on a date with him."

"Why doesn't she just go out with him? He's beautiful."

"She says she doesn't trust him; he's too good-looking."

"But he might be nice," suggested Lisa. "She should give him a chance."

"I agree, but Joe does have an awful reputation. That's the trouble with these players. They get a professional contract, and the girls come flocking. They sleep with a million of them, then when they meet a girl they like, they get upset when she won't take them seriously. Ask Matt about him, or Google him; he's got a rather colourful reputation. After what happened to you with Peter, we've all become a bit more cautious."

Lisa was struck by how much what had happened to her had affected everyone else in the family. "Peter was an ass," she said. "Just because he behaved like an idiot doesn't mean all guys will."

Emma nodded.

"Was it awful that I just disappeared and went off to Edinburgh when I discovered Peter was having an affair?" asked Lisa. "Hearing you talk like that makes me realize how tough it must have been."

"In the first week, it was terrible. We were all so worried. Do you remember that we all wanted to come out and see you and make sure you were OK, but you wouldn't let us? Deep down, I always thought you should have stayed and sorted things out with Peter, but I don't think that now. I think leaving was the best thing you could possibly have done; just look at you: you're happier and more confident than ever. Being with Charlie and away from any chance of bumping into Peter was the right decision. I love Charlie for taking you in and looking out for you like that. You need to get her to come and visit us soon. I owe her a beer or two."

From the seats behind them came an almighty scream. "Oooooooh…should have gone for a drop goal!" shouted her mom. "Well done forwards. Pity the backs are half-asleep. Oh no, hang on, here we go. Yes, yes, yes. A try!"

Lisa looked at her mother, clapping in delight. Really? Was she,

Lisa Lopez, the only person in this whole damn stadium who had no clue what was going on?

Lisa looked down at Matt, celebrating wildly, surrounded by cheerleaders in tiny bikini tops and the littlest skirts she'd ever seen. Was he one of the good guys? He certainly seemed it, but he was popular, and he might not be rich, but in the world of rugby, he was famous ...surely that gave him access to all sorts of beautiful women. She knew she had either to trust him or back off and not get involved, but it was difficult; seeing him standing there with these stunning girls brought back horrible memories of Peter.

She picked up her phone and called her sister at work. "Soph, can I ask you a favour? I know I was a pain and borrowed your lovely red dress and then didn't wear it, but can I borrow it tonight and wear it?"

"Of course," said Sophie. "You can borrow anything you want, any time. I've got some earrings that look lovely with it, and we must get Isabella working on your hair...the curls looked spectacular."

LISA FELT NERVOUS, excited and a little embarrassed as she walked into the sports bar for the post-game party. She never wore dresses, let alone a red one that clung to every curve.

Isabella and Sophia had been immensely proud of their handi-work, surveying and discussing Lisa as if she were a piece of art created by them. They had even high-fived each other, congratulating themselves heartily when she had walked into the room.

Now they were at the club, and Isabella took charge, leading the way through the packed bar to their corner spot, where Emma was on hand to wave them through to the VIP area. Lisa had been there for about five minutes, marvelling at the huge crowd that was already at the ticket-only party, when Matt spotted her.

"Good grief," he said, looking her up and down. "What happened?"

"I think you're supposed to say, 'you look lovely, Lisa,'" said Isabella. "But I guess that's what you mean."

"Yes, yes, of course. You look...well, different. I've always seen you as being quite casual and not a dressed-up sort of person, but you look beautiful. You always look beautiful."

Matt was dragged away by a smart-looking man in an impeccably-cut suit, leaving Isabella and Lisa at the bar. Sophia was surrounded by a gaggle of large, bearded rugby fans keen to make the acquaintance of the beautiful blonde with the astonishing figure.

"He likes you," said Isabella as soon as Matt was out of earshot. "The way he looks at you, the way he talks to you...he's crazy about you. Anyone can see it."

"Do you think so?" Lisa wasn't sure. Sometimes he was so loving and kind, then other times quite dismissive. Even his reaction to her just now was far from fulsome. She was dressed to the nines, looking better than she'd ever looked in her life before, and he didn't seem impressed. Perhaps he just didn't see her in that way. He thought about her as a friend, so he didn't notice or care a great deal whether she was all dressed up or all dressed down.

"He adores you," she said. "I'm absolutely sure of it. All you have to do is work out whether you're ready for a relationship."

"I definitely like him, but I hardly know him," she said. "And I want to believe that I'm ready for a relationship, but it's hard to know. How do you know whether you're ready?"

"By trying?" said Isabella. "By just throwing yourself into it and trusting it will work out."

"Maybe I should go and talk to him?" said Lisa.

"No, leave him for a minute. That guy who came over to talk to him is Steve Bence; he's on the board of Apple and their main sponsor. Matt probably needs to talk to him. Come with me; let's go and get you a large glass of wine."

The band came on as the evening progressed. Lisa and Isabella were joined by Sophia, then by Emma, who was released from bar duties to party with her sisters. The women kicked off their shoes and danced to tracks from the '70s and '80s. Matt hovered on the edge of the group until he stepped in and began dancing, twirling Lisa around and pulling her tightly to him. "Having fun," he said.

Lisa looked up at him, their eyes locked, in their own little world.

She felt so comfortable, so safe, so much like she wanted him to kiss her and hold her forever. They leaned in closer so their bodies were touching. She watched as he moved his head down so his lips were close to hers.

"Lisa?" The sound of her name being called broke through the tender moment. Then came a hand on her shoulder, and she was being turned around. She still felt warm and glowing from how close she'd just felt to Matt, how happy and excited she was at what could happen next between them.

"Peter?"

Her ex-fiancé, the love of her life, the man she thought she'd be with until they both died, was standing in front of her, smiling, with his hands on her shoulders. She felt her heart drop to her feet. He was looking into her eyes as if nothing had ever gone wrong, as if they were back three months ago, preparing for the amazing future they'd have together. As if he hadn't had the affair. He looked at her exactly like he always had. She looked back at him in confusion. What was he doing here? Why had he come to a rugby party? None of this made sense.

"You look amazing," he said. "I mean beautiful, incredible. Edinburgh suited you. Honestly, I've never seen you look so good."

Lisa just stared. It was the oddest moment. All in one minute, it was the one thing she'd wanted to happen for so long and the one thing she didn't want to happen at all.

"Thank you," she said, eventually. There were lots of questions burning away inside her, but none of them came out. She heard Matt's voice...lovely Matt, whom she might be kissing at this point had Peter not chosen to intervene.

"Everything OK?" he was asking. "Do you need me to do anything?"

"Yes!" Lisa wanted to scream. "Get this guy off me and come back and dance with me," but she couldn't. She felt rooted to the spot and unable to speak.

"I just need to talk to her," said Peter, looking over at Matt. Lisa noticed how tiny her ex-fiancé looked next to Matt. The last thing she wanted was a fight. She'd talk to Peter and tell him all the things she'd wanted to say for the past three months - get it all out of her system, tell him she was never coming back to him, then she'd go back to Matt and carry on dancing with him.

"I'll throw him out," said Matt.

"No, it's fine. Everything's fine. I'll talk to you later, Matt," she heard herself say. "I'll come back and find you later."

A look of pain and anguish swept across Matt's handsome face, and Lisa felt devastated, but what could she do? She needed to talk to Peter and sort this out for good. Then, she could allow herself to move on properly and consider a relationship with Matt.

But with painful timing, the band moved on to slow songs. The languid 80s hit, "Move Closer," drifted moodily through the air as couples moved onto the floor around them.

"Shall we dance?" Peter asked. Every instinct in her body wanted to tell him to go away; every fibre of her being screeched *ruuuuun*, but somehow she let him put his arms around her neck, and they started to dance.

"That's better, isn't it?" he asked, and it wasn't. This wasn't where she wanted to be at all. She saw Matt walk from the dance floor but still, she kept dancing. She didn't want to dance with Peter, but, at the same time, she didn't want *not* to dance with him. She wanted to talk to him and find out why he'd behaved the way he had. One of the problems with running off to Edinburgh was that she'd never confronted him. This was the man she was supposed to be spending the rest of her life with; she needed to find out why he'd thrown it all away.

"Let's go for a coffee," she said, moving out of his arms and over to get her coat. "Let's get out of here."

CHAPTER 6

"Please, tell me you're not going to get back with him," said Emma, plonking a cup of coffee in front of Lisa.

"No, of course not. No way. Why would you even think that?"

"Er...because you slow-danced with him all evening and ignored everyone else," said Sophia.

It was Sunday morning, and no one was working, so they were all free to interrogate her about the events of the night before.

"I know," said Lisa, blowing on her hot coffee. "I was just so shocked when he appeared. You don't know how difficult I find it even to hear his name, let alone find myself face-to-face with him. I froze. He kept saying how amazing I looked and how he regretted the way in which he'd behaved. It was like I was having this out-of-body experience. I didn't know what to do."

The girls sat in silence, looking at their sister. They wondered what was going on in her head.

"I told him that I wasn't interested and to keep away from me, then I got a taxi back on my own. I told him enough was enough, and it was over between us, and I came home. I couldn't have come back inside; I was shaking too much. I don't want that man anywhere near me."

"OK. I'm just saying it looked like you were going to get back with him."

"What does it matter what it looked like?" asked Lisa. She knew why she was being so defensive, and she knew what they were think-ing...that Matt had seen Peter and her dancing.

"And if you're all worried about Matt, you can stop now. I told you that he and I are just friends...there's nothing else going on. I'm too hurt by Peter to even think about another relationship. I'm going to my room."

She didn't exactly flounce out, but she did hold her head high and walk with some pace, slamming her bedroom door behind her before collapsing on the bed. On her phone, there were texts from Peter...more texts. The last one said that they should go out to dinner so that they could talk. She replied that she wasn't interested several times, but he didn't give up easily. She was a challenge; she was a target. Peter was such an uncompromising alpha male that he would now put up a huge fight to get her back out of sheer spite and pride. And what if he got her back? He'd probably do exactly the same thing again. She wouldn't give him that chance.

"Lisa," Emma popped her head around Lisa's bedroom door and saw her lying there, staring at the ceiling.

"Are you OK? It must be really difficult, just seeing him like that. Look, no one blames you for running out. We're all on your side, OK?"

"Thank you," Lisa said. "It's not easy just to forget him and start again with someone else, especially not when he appeared like that. It's going to take me time."

"I know. I do understand. Have you heard from him since last night?"

"I've had lots of texts from him."

"Saying what?" asked Emma, sitting on the edge of the bed.

"Oh, just that he regrets everything, wishes we were still together, can't wait to see me again...stuff like that."

"Mmmm...have you replied?"

"Yes, I've told him that I'm not interested."

"He'll get the message eventually," said Emma. "And in the mean-time, if you need anything - just shout."

"Sure," said Lisa. "There is something. I need to go and see Nancy to apologize for running out on her and to find out whether there is any way I can get my job back. You wouldn't come with me, would you?"

"Of course. When do you want to go?" said Emma.

"In about half an hour?"

"No problem. You get yourself ready, and we'll go. Don't wear the red dress; it causes chaos!"

"Ha, ha, ha," said Lisa. "You're so funny."

At least she could try to get her job back and bring some direction to her life. After that, she could work out what she was going to do about this "two men" situation she seemed to have inadvertently created for herself. There was rich and sophisticated Peter, who had broken her heart, and lovely Matt, who wanted to put her together again. She knew which one would make her happier...Matt - every time, but she had to cut off all feelings for Peter first. She needed to get him completely out of her head and get herself to a position where she didn't collapse when he walked into the room.

It was strange driving down the long driveway to Suffolk Manor. She'd done it so many times before, always thinking through what needed to be done that day, what plans she had for her staff, and how she could make the gardens look more beautiful. She was always striving to improve the way the place looked. This time he sat back and admired it all...the spectacular shrubs, the passion flowers and black-eyed Susan flowers crawling up over the trellis they'd spent days erecting. Everything she'd set in motion had burst into flower.

"Wow," she said to Emma. "It looks amazing."

'I know. It always does. All because of your hard work."

"I'd forgotten just how lovely it all looks. I mean - it's beautiful. This might be the first time I've truly appreciated how lovely it is here."

It wasn't just the general gardening she'd been in charge of when she worked at the Manor; she was in charge of making sure all the grounds looked perfect for particular events, so when she was making decisions about planting, in the back of her mind she'd know when the Spring Ball took place, when the Valentine's Ball was, when the big summer balls were staged and when there would be dignitaries visiting, so she could make sure that the garden was in full bloom for those key occasions.

As they drove along, Lisa realized that it was the Summer Ball coming up, and she wondered whether her replacement at the house would be aware of just how much work she had done to make sure that all the plants were perfect by the time the visitors swept through the front doors in all their finery. She hoped that the system she had implemented was being adhered to. She'd hate it if the place didn't look wonderful for Nancy on her big day.

Lisa felt nervous when they arrived at the front door. "What if she's mad with me?" she said to Emma. "I did disappear suddenly; she might be cross."

Emma put an arm around her shoulders encouragingly. "Relax. Explain everything. She'll understand."

"Christ, I hope she doesn't hate me," said Lisa. "She'd have every reason to."

Most of all, Lisa hoped that Nancy would give her her job back. She needed some focus in her life and to be doing something that mattered to her and didn't involve either Matt or Peter. Something that was hers. Something she cared about.

Bernard opened the door, and his eyes lit up when he saw Lisa. "Wow. Lovely to see you. I thought you disappeared for good," he said, smiling at her. "Come in, come in. Nancy will be delighted to see you."

"You remember my sister Emma, don't you?" said Lisa.

"Of course, I remember, Emma. You're in charge of that new sports bar now, aren't you? I hear wonderful things about it."

"Thank you, yes. It's an amazing place," said Emma. "We all have a lot of fun there."

"You see, you've missed all this," said Bernard. "You missed the arrival of this amazing rugby team and the buzz that's created. There "are gorgeous rugby players all over the place. That's a lot for an old man like me to handle."

"Yes, I know," said Lisa. "Very easy on the eye, aren't they? I've just been catching up on everything I missed."

Lisa could hear Nancy in the background and the sound of her shoes as she clip-clopped through the house. Even in her own home, she was immaculately dressed, always in cream, always looking aristocratic and sophisticated. Bernard swung the door a little wider so that Nancy could see who her guest was.

"My God, you're back." Nancy swung her arms around Lisa joyously, held her hand and led her into the house. "Are you OK? I was so worried about you. You just disappeared. I heard the rumours that you were in Scotland somewhere. It was all so dreadful. How are you now?"

"I'm fine," said Lisa. "I just wanted to apologize for disappearing. It was bad of me not to come and see you, but I was so hurt and upset; I just ran away. It was the silliest thing to do…"

"Don't be crazy, of course it wasn't a silly thing to do. I'm sure it was the best thing to do at that moment. I heard all about what happened; dreadful, horrible little man. But I'm glad you're back and looking so well. I don't suppose you want your job back, do you?"

"Oh my God, more than anything. I'd love to have my old job back."

"Well, that's fixed. We never did replace you, and with the Ball coming up in weeks, we are desperate. When can you start?"

"How about tomorrow?" asked Lisa.

"Perfect. It's a deal. We'll see you in the morning. There is something I should tell you, though… I'm not going to be staying here too much longer. I'm selling the house, and I'm going to move somewhere a little smaller, nearer to my sister. So, you'll have a new boss at some point."

"I knew you were going," said Lisa. "When do you think it will be?"

"We've only just found a buyer, and he seems in no great rush to move, so I will take it slowly and find somewhere perfect before heading off. I guess I will be gone in about six months?"

"Well, I will miss you enormously," said Lisa. "You've been the most fantastic person to work for, and I'm so grateful to you for giving me a second chance."

"Don't mention it," said Nancy. "In any case, I'm sure the new person will be lovely to work for. He seems an absolute delight."

"He might not want to keep me on," said Lisa. "He might come with his own head gardener, or his wife might have other ideas about how she wants things to look."

"I don't think there's any wife around, as far as I can see," said Nancy. "And he hasn't mentioned wanting to get rid of the staff. I will highly recommend you to him, and I'll tell him he'd be insane to get rid of you."

Lisa and Emma kissed Nancy on the cheek and left the big house. They skipped arm-in-arm as they went back to the car; Lisa was thrilled and delighted that her job was hers once again. She was concerned that a new owner was about to take over and may get rid of her, but all she could do was work as hard as possible and be as good as she possibly could, then hope that the new guy wanted her when he bought the house.

BACK AT HOME, Lisa was restless. She kind of missed Matt. Not romantically, of course. She missed the casual friendship they'd had. She missed their chats and the funny texts he used to send. It was like there was something missing, as if the light had been turned down.

It bothered her that she seemed to have upset him so much. Surely he understood how complicated it was for her when Peter walked in that evening? They all lived in a small town. She was bound to bump into him at some point. Sure, it was a bloody shame that it had happened while she was in Matt's arms, but there wasn't much she could have done about the timing. It's not like she'd asked Peter to walk in. But Matt was ignoring her, so that was that.

Later that afternoon, walking along the beach with Emma, both aiming to blow away their hangovers, Lisa decided to confide in her sister. "You know, Matt has completely ignored me all day," she said.

"He's just upset," said Emma.

"Have you spoken to him?"

"Last night I did. He likes you. He was sad that this guy who'd broken your heart came in, and you rushed off with him."

"That's not fair," said Lisa. "I didn't rush off with him; I rushed home alone."

"Then all you have to do is tell Matt that," said Emma. "If you're interested in him."

"I do like him, Emms, but I don't know whether I'm read. I was engaged to Peter. The man broke my heart, for God's sake. I can't just forget that whole part of my life. Matt knows how injured I was."

"Matt will understand. But be careful with him. If you're not interested in him, please tell him."

"I am interested. I like him, Emms, but I'm scared. I don't want to get hurt. I think that he and I should just stay friends for now."

"For now," said Emma, with a smile. "Who knows what the future holds? Anyway, what did Peter have to say for himself? Anything interesting?"

"I didn't give him much of a chance. I just wanted to get away," said Lisa. "He was running after me while I was running out of the club and trying to get an uber. He shouted that he loved me and wanted me back. He phoned me every day when I first got to Edinburgh, and he wanted to remind me of that. He kept saying it was a one-off, everyone makes mistakes, and he wanted to be given another chance."

"I'm sure he regrets what he did because he lost you and the dancer, and now he's on his own, but it doesn't change the fact that he was an absolute shit and broke your heart."

CHAPTER 7

here was something both deliciously familiar and horribly challenging about going back to her job after a three-month absence. Lisa climbed out of the car and pulled on her wellington boots, grabbed her gloves and headed toward the back of the big house where the workmen, gardeners and other outside workers were based. There was a big shed there containing all the equipment they used, as well as access to the huge conservatory where they could sit and relax after shifts or during lunch times. The two huge sheepdogs—Molly and Dolly—would rush around them, licking their hands in a bid for scraps.

Nothing had changed about the setup at the back of the house, of course; the only thing that had changed was Lisa herself, but she would not let her confusion about Matt and Peter affect her work. She zipped up her coat, looked at the agenda that had been put together for her approval, and prepared to issue instructions for the day.

The last time she'd been working at the house, she had been looking forward to her and Peter finally setting a date for their wedding. How innocent that time seemed now; how naive she'd been.

She'd had no idea that it was all going to crumble into dust and fly away on the breeze.

"Welcome back, sweetheart," said Tom, the big, burly gardener who had been working there since before Lisa was born. He would set about his work with such a plodding slowness that she had wondered whether he ever got anything done. But at the end of every day, when she went around and checked, everything was in order; what he'd been working on was always done perfectly. He understood the land; he understood how nature worked, and he was an absolute joy to work with.

LISA GATHERED the equipment that she needed for the day; she was planning to work on the areas around the long pathway leading to the house to make it look as beautiful as possible for the Summer Ball in two weeks. She put all her equipment into the wheelbarrow and pushed it along the path toward the area she had assigned for herself, near the fountain and, therefore, likely to catch the eyes of the guests.

As she got to work, weeding and checking that the plants were all looking good, she heard footsteps coming down the path toward her.

"It's so lovely to have you back," said Nancy, pulling her to her feet and hugging her. "What on earth are you doing weeding? You're the head gardener; you're supposed to be in charge of this unruly mob."

"I just thought I'd start small, you know, take a look around, get involved in some basic gardening, then sort everything out after my shift and make sure I'm fully on top of what's going on."

"Whatever you think is best. But remember, you're in charge."

The day passed quickly, as it always did when she was in the gardens; she spent the afternoon walking around, familiarizing herself with everyone and everything, and checking that nothing terrible had happened while she'd been away. The only problem seemed to be with the three large cherry trees at the back of the far garden. They had lost a couple of branches in the Easter storms. She made a note that the wayward branches needed to be moved and taken away. Then she wandered back through the grass, thinking to herself how totally happy she was when she was here, more so than anywhere else in the world.

She'd made herself keep her phone in her car while she was at work, checking it only on her breaks so that she didn't become obsessed with the fact that Matt was not returning her calls. When she switched it on, it showed three missed calls, all from Peter.

Lisa went through to the big house to get herself cleaned up and to say goodbye to Nancy before heading off for the evening. She was going to meet Emma and Isabella for a drink; then they were all going to a fashion show at Sophia's shop. Lisa wasn't remotely interested in fashion, but she wanted to support Sophia, and, rather excitingly, Matt was supposed to be there. She might finally get to see him.

Lisa was brushing her hair in the mirror when Nancy walked into the large bathroom and sat on the small velvet chair next to her.

"You have the most beautiful hair," she said. "It always looks perfect. I'm very envious of how lovely and long it is"

"Thank you," Lisa replied, unable to mask the sound of surprise in her voice. "I never think of myself as having nice hair. I'm no good at doing anything with it. Isabella gets mad at me for never making an effort."

"You don't need to do anything with it. It's gorgeous as it is. You're lucky. With that amazing hair, beautiful face and stunning figure, you don't need to worry. Just wait until you get to my age; everything falls apart, and you must spend an hour putting yourself together before you're fit to face other people...or even the dogs! Molly is terrified of me first thing. Heavens, I'm terrified of myself first thing!"

"Nonsense," said Lisa. "You always look so lovely, so well put-together. I feel like such a scruff next to you."

"My dear, don't ever feel scruffy next to anyone. Men will always prefer someone naturally pretty. They want someone who takes great joy from the world and is full of love and compassion, not someone artificial, closed and unapproachable. Just mark my words. You'll always have men falling at your feet, just because you're you."

"That's such a lovely thing to say. Thank you."

"You're very welcome. I suppose what I'm saying is that Peter is a damn fool, and he'll live to regret the way he behaved. Lots of men will be beating a path to your door, I'm sure."

"Mmmm…I'm a bit off men at the moment, after what happened, but I appreciate the compliment."

"Oh, forget about him, dear. He's not worth another thought. Did you know I bumped into him soon after you left for Edinburgh?"

"No, I hadn't heard," said Lisa. "What did you say?"

"He came up to me and said, 'good morning,' like there was nothing wrong. I told him I thought he was the scum of the earth, and I wished him a very bad morning, really the worst sort of morning for a person to have. He looked shocked."

Lisa's hand shot up to her mouth to stifle a giggle. Nancy was

"And that woman was with him," Nancy continued. "She was very plain, you know. I growled at her: 'You should be ashamed of yourself,' I said. She looked quite terrified. They shuffled off then. I haven't seen either of them since."

TWO HOURS LATER, Lisa found herself in the peculiar position of sitting in the front row of a fashion show. Not her usual habitat by any means, but she was surprised to find herself enjoying it. The drama and excitement were captivating, and it was so good to see Sophia taking centre stage. She looked completely in her element as she air-kissed designers and swept around the room beautifully and with such elegance.

Lisa felt a rush of pride. She sometimes felt that she and her sister weren't from the same species, let alone the same family. Sophia was the most ethereal creature, while Lisa always felt solid, dependable and down-to-earth, like a friendly, reliable family dog. Sophia was the opposite…like a swan, gliding around the room with this alluring air of fragility and quiet confidence.

"Now, ladies and gentlemen, please would you put your hands together and offer a warm welcome to our special guests…the wonderful, all-winning, all-handsome and all-gorgeous Salcombe Sharks rugby team."

Lisa held her breath; would Matt be there? Sophia said she had invited him and had hoped he would come but that he hadn't confirmed.

Lisa cupped her hand around her face in excitement as a huge cheer rang out from the predominantly female crowd, then out walked three of the players, striding down the makeshift catwalk, buffed to perfection and wearing nothing but shorts. The crowd went wild, and the players looked at one another, seeking solidarity in this most peculiar of situations. Lisa tried to work out which players they were. She was on the verge of deciding that she didn't know them when one of the men ran over to Sophia, lifted her up, kissed her on the cheek and ran back. It was Joe. How could she have missed him?

Next, it was the turn of players in smart clothes to make an appearance; Lisa spotted Will and Ted at the start of the catwalk, ready to walk on. They wore beautifully cut suits and exceptionally classy ties and had glamorous handkerchiefs tucked nattily into their top pockets. They walked up the catwalk looking half-embarrassed and half-thrilled while the audience cheered them every step of the way. It was all great fun in every way except one - Matt was nowhere to be seen.

The final stage was dinner jackets, and Joe was back on the catwalk looking Hollywood gorgeous in his black tie. He was joined by Will. Lisa nudged Emma as he sauntered along. "Very nice," she said under her breath.

"He's all man," replied Emma. 'My lovely friend Will looking super hot."

The truth was that they all looked hot. The photographers were in overdrive, snapping away furiously. The pictures would be all over the papers and the websites in the morning, helping Sophia to get lots of publicity for the shop. It was an out-and-out triumph.

"We have the cleverest sister in the world," said Lisa, while Emma sat there, quietly lost in a trance at the sights she'd just witnessed.

"Is Matt coming tonight?" Isabella asked Lisa.

"I don't know. Sophia said he was coming, but there's no sign of him. I was hoping to be able to talk to him."

"Have you not heard anything from him?"

"Nothing at all. He hasn't returned my calls or answered any of my texts. Just won't talk to me after Saturday night."

"He's coming," said Emma, leaning over to join the conversation. "He offered me a lift home earlier, so I know he's here somewhere. I'm just off to mingle for a while. Back in a minute."

"Will you text me if you see him? Or try and persuade him to come and talk to me?" Lisa shouted after her, raising her voice above the din of the screaming woman.

"Of course," said her sister, kissing her on the cheek.

Lisa looked such a mess, but suddenly she didn't care. Buoyed by Nancy's kind words earlier and motivated by a sudden eagerness to see him, she didn't care if she wasn't all wrapped up in an elegant dress or hadn't had her hair curled by her clever sister. She just wanted to see him. She liked him. He made her feel happy. Wasn't that all that mattered?

As she picked at her fingernails, nervously looking around in the hope of catching sight of him, she noticed Isabella watching her.

"You like him, don't you?" she said.

"Kind of," said Lisa. "I've been kidding myself that it's all too soon, and I want to take it slowly, but I've missed not talking to him."

"Well, let's go find him then," said Isabella. "Let's sort this out."

"OK," said Lisa nervously, following her sister.

They wandered around the room, past the most immaculately dressed people in Devon, all out in force in their finest clothes. Every time Lisa saw a tall, dark man, her heart beat a little faster, but none of them was Matt. He was nowhere to be seen.

They found Emma in the corner of the room, drinking a can of beer while everyone around her elegantly sipped champagne. She was deep in conversation with Joe. From what they could hear, he was asking about Sophia and whether the glamorous fashionista would ever go out with him. Emma was offering words of reassurance. "Give her time; she'll say yes eventually...she's only human."

Emma had such a great bond with these players. They treated her like a sister, chatting with her freely and sharing their concerns. Lisa knew that she could never be like that. She was too private—too shy. She liked people and enjoyed being around them but hated being the centre of attention, and she preferred meeting people one-on-one rather than in a large group. And there was just one person she wanted to meet one-to-one right now.

"Have you seen Matt anywhere?" she asked Emma.

"He decided not to come," said Emma. "I've tried to call him, but he's not picking up. Try calling him?"

Lisa's heart sank. There was no point in calling or texting him. But she missed him. She wanted their friendship back. If she was honest with herself, she wanted more than friendship, but she'd probably completely blown any chance of that.

CHAPTER 8

The week went past in a blur of flowers, trees and planning. With just over a week to go before the Summer Ball, there was a lot to do if the place was going to look perfect. The planting had been done before she went away, but the lack of organization while she'd been in Scotland, meant that not all of the plants had been tended to properly. Many of them simply wouldn't look good enough for the party.

Painstakingly, she removed the plants from the conservatory and took the plants already in the conservatory to replant outside. By the end of the week, she was much happier. She hadn't had to throw away any plants—all the ones that were dying had been put on life support in the conservatory, and all the plants outside would look fantastic by the time the party came around. It had been tough but exhilarating. She would have hated to throw any plants away—to her, that would be like drowning kittens. They'd all been rescued, and all was well.

When Saturday came, Lisa could think of nothing but the game. She was dying to go along and see Matt. Perhaps if she could just see and smile at him, he'd smile back, and their friendship could start again. She missed him. She missed his warmth, his kindness and his friendliness. She missed everything about him. But she didn't want to go to the match when everything was so difficult between them.

Her sisters all went to the game, of course: Emma wearing her Sharks scarf and shirt, and Isabella in a rather attractive cape and black pants that Sophia had managed to get for her with a hefty discount. Issy was so paranoid about her weight that her sartorial decisions were directed by her need to cover up. Lisa thought she worried too much; she was a very attractive girl.

When she walked in, their father sat up and looked at her. "Fancy dress party is it? Going as Batman?"

"Ha, ha, ha," said Isabella. "You're so funny."

Then, when Sophia walked in wearing a beautiful burgundy pair of loose pants and a matching top, he continued, "Ahh...here's Robin. Have fun at the game, Batman and Robin."

The girls kissed their parents goodbye and checked with Lisa that she was sure she didn't want to come.

"No, I've got an awful headache," she said as they headed out to the car. "I'll just hang out at home today."

"Are you sure you don't want to go with them?" asked her mum. "Not like you to sit at home."

"No, I don't feel like it, not with this headache. I think I'll have an early night."

"Your father and I are getting a takeaway later," her mum added.

"Perfect," said Lisa. She'd go for a walk along the beach and then spend the evening at home with her mum and dad. That would be good. It would be safer. She couldn't bear the idea of more rejection... especially not from Matt, and she didn't want to bump into Peter again. Her home was the safest place to be.

Strolling along the beach always made her think of her childhood. That was the thing about living in one place your whole life; it was impossible to avoid seeing things and thinking of things that took you back twenty years. She thought of the rocks that she and her sisters scrambled over, hunting for crabs and looking for lovely seashells and fascinating rock pools, while Sophia stood on the edge, keen to be involved but far from keen to get dirty or grubby.

She smiled as she remembered Sophia hovering, looking immaculate in her matching jacket and boots. She could only have been about seven, but even then, she was a fashionista. Their father would try to tempt her onto the rocks to join them, but Sophia was not having any of it. She lingered on the edge—as she so often had done in their childhood, very clear of who she was and what she wanted. She hated getting dirty and didn't feel happy unless she was properly dressed and looking her best. How lovely that the family had always appreciated Sophia for what she was and allowed her to be herself. Look where she was now—doing a job she loved with huge potential—happy, confident and secure. The same went for all of them. They had been allowed to be themselves and live the lives they wanted to live —always.

MONDAY MORNING FLEW AROUND, and Lisa was back where she belonged. Well, not quite where she belonged—she was in the kitchen at Suffolk House with Nancy rather than in the garden, but at least they were discussing the garden. Nancy wanted to know all the arrangements for the Ball. Lisa had strong views; she'd been working there for four years and remembered how the gardens had been laid out for each ball. She knew when the garden had looked its best and was keen for Nancy to replicate the best garden designs from the past.

"How about if we have fairy lights through the circle of trees and around the side of the house, with spotlights onto the pathway, highlighting the flowers."

"Yes, perfect," said Nancy. Lisa had a feeling that Nancy would say yes to whatever she suggested; the lady of the house had such faith in her.

"I'll make it beautiful," said Lisa as the doorbell rang. Lisa scribbled thoughts and notes onto the plans in front of her while Nancy moved toward the entrance hall to greet her visitor.

"We should have the coloured lights through the rose garden as well," said Lisa. "Lots of people wander down there during the evening. It would be nice to light it in that soft-pink colour."

"Lisa, have you met Matt?" asked Nancy, bringing Matt into the kitchen with her arms around him. "He's my favourite rugby coach in the whole world."

"Hi, um, yes, we've, um—we've met," said Lisa, feeling her cheeks scorch with embarrassment and her heart beat a little faster. Gosh, he was lovely. She'd forgotten just how incredibly attractive he was. He looked nervous to see her, which made him look even more appealing.

"We've met before. How are you, Lisa?" asked Matt, leaning in to kiss her.

Her cheeks were hot; she knew she looked wildly embarrassed.

"That's good; I'm glad you two know one another. Now, let's have coffee, shall we? Matt, Lisa's running through the plans for the garden at the Ball. What were you saying, Lisa? Perhaps Matt has a view on it all."

"Sure, fire away," said Matt. He was standing right next to her. Her heart was racing a million miles an hour.

"Well, um. These are the plans…"

"Looks good," said Matt. He was looking directly at her, but she looked down. She didn't want to catch his eye.

"What were you saying about the rose garden?"

"Oh, just that people tend to wander down there, so we should make it look perfect."

"I see. Yes, sounds good. Do people go down there after dancing?"

"Yes," said Nancy, joining them at the table. "To cool down after particularly ferocious dancing or to get up to no good at all."

"So, might be the sort of place you'd go after dancing with your ex-boyfriend or something? Although, no – strike that – most normal people wouldn't go dancing with their ex-boyfriend, would they?"

"I suppose they might," said Lisa. "If their ex-boyfriend, who they hadn't seen for ages, just started dancing with them, and they were too stunned to stop him. It might be somewhere a girl would go if she wanted to escape from the ex because she wasn't interested in him."

"But if a girl wasn't interested in her ex, why would she dance with him? Especially if there was another man standing on the sidelines, who liked her and was trying to make that clear?"

"Presumably because the girl was thrown by the arrival of the ex. People do odd things when they panic. At least the girl went home alone. And how about if the man hovering on the sidelines should have made it more obvious that he liked the girl? And, if he did like her, why would he refuse to talk to her for ages afterwards and ignore the girl's messages and calls? Imagine how that made the girl feel when all she was doing was panicking."

"You've got to think about it from the man's point of view," said Matt. "If a man likes someone and is dancing with her, he would feel slightly put out if that girl then went off with her ex."

"Went off with? I think the ex grabbed the girl and left her little choice other than to dance with him. Once the girl could get away from the ex, she did, and she went home alone. I think the man should apologize to the girl for behaving like a jerk."

"The girl should apologise to the man for making him feel freaking awful."

"The girl apologises."

"So does the man," said Matt.

The two smiled at one another while Nancy poured coffee. "Good. Right. Well, that's sorted out then. Let's have lights in the rose garden." she said, confusion across her face.

CHAPTER 9

*J*t was the oddest way to reconcile, but it seemed to have worked. Within minutes of Matt leaving, Lisa had a text from him. "Dinner tonight? Pick you up at 7:00?"

"See you then," she replied.

It was 6:30 p.m. when she heard him pull up outside the house. She had decided to play it cool and be herself. No fancy dresses from Sophia, no curly hair from Isabella, just her and her rather dull wardrobe. If that wasn't good enough, then this relationship would never work. Matt wasn't flash - he had barely two dimes to rub together - she'd go for a much more natural look.

Lisa loved the fact that, though he arrived at 6:30, he waited outside until just before 7:00 before knocking. There was something very sweet and kind about that. Luckily, none of her sisters was in. Sophia had gone to the cinema with the girls from work; Isabella was working late at a hairdressing college, teaching the hairstylists of the future and earning herself a few quid in the process; and Emma was at a meeting with the club's executives to plan how they would organise a program of social events during the closed season. They were very keen for the club to continue to attract fans and socialisers when the season was over. A program of great events would surely achieve that. Only her mum and dad were in the house.

Lisa heard the joy in her mum's voice as she answered the door.

"Matt, how lovely to see you," she said. "Donald, look who it is; Matt's popped in to say hello. Put the kettle on, would you, dear? Or perhaps you'd prefer something stronger? A beer? Donald, get Matt a beer."

"I've come to pick up Lisa, actually," said Matt. "So, I won't stop for a drink now, but I'll be back soon to relieve you of one of those beers."

"Oh, right, OK. Lisa. Yes—I'll just get her."

Lisa hadn't spoken to her parents about Matt at all. There hadn't seemed to be any need. They had a lovely friendship, which might have gone further, but then the arrival of Peter had somehow put an end to that; now they were just going out for a quiet dinner to catch up.

Her mom knocked gently on her door. "Matt's here," she said.

Lisa swung the door open and gave her mom a hug. "We're just popping out for something to eat," she said. "We won't be long."

"Aren't you going to get changed?" asked her mom.

"I have changed," said Lisa. She had showered and washed her hair, and she looked pretty acceptable in her pale pink jumper and cropped jeans with white tennis-style pumps. She was much more dressed up than she had planned to be. At one point, she'd thought about going out in her work gear.

But, when she walked into the living room, she understood why her mom had asked; Matt was there, dressed to the nines. He had a suit and tie on, a really lovely, expensive-looking suit with an immaculate white shirt and an elegant tie. He looked like one of the models on the runway at Sophia's fashion show.

"You look great," said Lisa, unable to hide her surprise. "I'm completely underdressed."

"No, no, you're not. You look perfect," said Matt. "Now, come on— I'm starving; let's go and eat."

They headed to a small seafood restaurant right on the beach, not in Cove Bay, where they would be seen by everyone and gossiped about relentlessly, but further down the coast, where she knew fewer people. "I still can't get over how good you look," said Lisa, as Matt threw his jacket over the back of his seat. It had a red silk lining that perfectly matched his tie. How had he afforded such an expensive suit?

"Thanks. After seeing you in that red dress, I thought I'd better up my game," he said. "You, looking like a supermodel, and the big-city lawyer arriving in his perfect suit, with his perfect hair. Arrogant prick."

"He is an arrogant prick," said Lisa. "I loved him once, but I don't love him now."

"Good. But did you think you would fall for him again when you saw him?"

"No, of course not," she said. "I mean, I knew I'd bump into him somewhere, at some point, but I didn't think for one minute that I'd want to go off with him."

"Did you know he'd be coming to the party last week?"

"No, of course not. I wouldn't have gone if I thought he'd turn up."

"Oh. I thought you must have invited him. I assumed that's why you'd arrived all dressed up and looking amazing. I thought you'd planned to meet him there."

"No, no, no. You've got this all wrong," said Lisa. "I got dressed up for you, not him. I had no idea he would be there. I was completely thrown when he walked in, and he was dancing with me before I knew what had happened. The last time I'd seen him, he'd been screwing someone on his desk and wrecking our relationship. Suddenly, he was there, and I was frozen to the spot. How could you think that I'd arranged to meet him there?"

"I don't know," said Matt. "I just assumed you'd thought about it and decided you wanted to be with him."

"You've got this all wrong, so wrong," said Lisa. "Completely wrong. We need a new word for wrong."

"Well, make sure you don't wear that super-sexy red dress again; that threw me completely. When we'd been out, you'd always looked so fresh-faced and lovely, then suddenly you were dressed to kill."

"For you!" she repeated. "Because I liked you, not because of my fucking ex-boyfriend."

Matt held her hand over the table and gave it a gentle squeeze.

"For the record, even though you looked lovely that day, I prefer you like this...all natural."

"Good," she said. "Though I do like you in that suit. I expect you to look like that every time we meet."

"Mmmm," he said, unconvinced. "I have a confession to make about this suit...I borrowed it from Sophia. When you said you would come out tonight, I called her and asked her whether I could borrow the suit that I was supposed to model at the fashion show. I'd only agreed to be in the show because you'd be there, and I had this sudden thought that you'd turn up with Peter, so I backed out."

"Ahhhh..." said Lisa, as she thought back to the night of the show and how she'd been eager to talk to him.

"Can you just promise me one thing?" she asked. "Any more mix-ups or confusions, talk to me."

"I could try that," he said. "But I'm a guy; remember, I'm not the best of communicators."

THEY DROVE BACK to Lisa's house rather than to Matt's apartment, which he'd admitted was cramped and unattractive. But when they got back, the constraints imposed by three sisters and two parents appearing at the front door were too off-putting, even for the most amorous of pursuers.

"I'll call you tomorrow," he said, kissing her tenderly on the cheek.

"OK," she said, skipping out of the car and hearing the groans of disappointment from her parents and sisters when they realised he wasn't coming in. Matt didn't wait until morning to contact her; he texted right away, then called her when he got home. She went to bed filled with a sense of well-being and happiness that she hadn't felt since...well, since ever.

CHAPTER 10

"Someone's got a spring in her step this morning." Georgina smiled as she watched her youngest daughter sashay jauntily to breakfast and poured herself a bowl of cereal.

"Well, I had a good night last night. I've got a great job, a lovely family...life is pretty good." Lisa kissed her mum on the top of her head and sat at the table. She was leaving much earlier than her sisters, so the rest of the house was bathed in silence as the two of them sat down to breakfast.

"Matt's a nice guy; I've always had a soft spot for him. But do remember that you are not long out of that relationship with dreadful Peter. I'd hate for you to rush into anything."

"Don't worry, Mum. I'm taking it very slowly. Honestly, don't worry. We're just good friends."

That wasn't strictly true. They had shared a kiss after leaving the restaurant and would have shared a few more had they not returned to the house to find the whole family at home.

"Good. You've been through so much. I'd hate for you to start with someone else too soon."

"I won't," said Lisa.

. . .

IT WAS A BEAUTIFUL, warm summer's day, perfect for being outside, so Lisa decided to launch herself at the rose garden. Everything needed to look perfect before the summer ball, but nowhere more than this paradise of colours and scents. When it was looking its best, it sang and shone. It was a real jewel in the garden that attracted people to it as if magnetised.

Lisa began by checking all the buds, then looked at what weeding was needed, writing down all the tasks that had to be done. It wasn't something that one person could do; she needed a couple of them to work on it this afternoon.

"Can I interrupt you?" asked a male voice as she tore off dead rosebuds.

Lisa turned around.

"Hello," she said, alarmed to see Matt standing in front of her with his hands pushed deep into his trouser pockets. "How are you this morning?"

"I'm amazing, thank you," said Matt. "Anyone would think I had a date with a girl I liked last night."

He walked towards her as he spoke and took her head in his hands. "There was only one thing missing last night, and that was not being able to kiss you when I dropped you off...I didn't want to give a performance in front of your entire family, so I drove off. It's been annoying me ever since."

Lisa smiled, embarrassed.

"So, I thought I'd come and find you and give you that kiss now."

"OK," she said nervously. "But I'm not dressed for romance...."

"Oh well," he said as he kissed her gently, then pulled her towards him, kissing her more deeply.

"Well...that was nice," he said as they parted. "Can I do that again?"

"Yes, please," said Lisa, with a smile.

They kissed once more; then he hugged her so tightly she thought he would break her in two. He lifted her off the ground and spun her around, putting her down and kissing her on the cheek. "You're lovely. I don't suppose you can get away for lunch, can you?"

"I can't," said Lisa. "I'm having lunch with Nancy to discuss plans for the Rose Garden. That's what I'm trying to work out now."

"OK," he said, dismay creeping across his face. "Never mind. I've been invited to your house for dinner tonight, so I'll see you then...."

"Invited over to my house?"

"Yep, I saw Emma earlier with your mum, and they asked me whether I could bring back the barbecue that Joe borrowed a while back...we had a barbie on the beach when the team first arrived. Anyway, I told them I'd bring it back later, and they told me to stay for something to eat. Is that OK?"

"Yes, it's more than OK," she said. "It's wonderful. I'll see you later."

Matt smiled and gave a mock salute as he turned to go. She watched him walk to his car, loving the way he kept turning to look at her. Once he reached his car and drove away, down the long driveway towards the main road, she returned to the roses and her faithful notebook.

She had to trim the flowers so they sat back from the path and people didn't cut themselves or snag clothing on them. She'd do that straight away, then work on the roses on the trellises at the back. As she reached for her secateurs, she thought of Matt coming for dinner that evening. A shiver of delight ran through her. She couldn't remember the last time she'd felt this happy.

7 PM CAME, and the family was gathered in the garden. The barbecue was lit, and it was the usual story: the men fussed over the meat while the women rushed around in the kitchen, doing the real work... preparing salads, making sure the beef was tenderised correctly and ready for barbecuing, and preparing sauces and condiments while checking on the baked potatoes and buttering rolls for the burgers and hot dogs.

It was strange for Lisa to stand there, watching the scene unfolding in front of her. She'd only had one proper date with Matt, but it was like he was part of the family because he had got to know the family before he got to know her. It was weird but rather lovely that she wouldn't have to go through the painful process of introducing him to everyone.

"All the rolls ready yet?" asked Matt, plates in both hands full of burgers.

"Right on it," said Lisa, wandering through the patio doors into the kitchen and kicking off her flip-flops by the door before reaching for the massive platter of buttered rolls. She was still in the habit of kicking her flip-flops off every time she came in from the beach, having been told a million times through her childhood that shoes worn on the beach should not be worn in the house, or the house would be full of sand, and she would be responsible for cleaning it all up.

She took the salads and sauces out with her, and Emma followed close behind, clutching cheese and hot dog rolls.

"Here you go, chef," said Lisa, putting the platter down and opening one of the rolls so he could slide in a rather delicious-looking burger. "I think I might keep this one for myself."

She arranged a plate full of burgers, filled them with cheese, pickles and slices of crispy bacon that they had cheated and prepared in the oven, and handed them around with handfuls of crisps and salad, promising everyone that potatoes and hot dogs were also on the way.

"This is fantastic," said Emma, looking at Matt. "The food is delicious, and it's been prepared by my boss. Matt, I think you should do this more often."

"Ha, ha," said Matt. "Don't get too used to this sort of treatment. This is a one-off."

"Come and join us," Lisa said to Matt. He'd been sitting next to her dad all evening, helping with the cooking.

"Donald, are you OK over there if I join these ladies for a quick drink?" Matt shouted over as he grabbed his bottle of beer.

"Oh, I see; I've been deserted, have I?"

"Not at all. I'll be back as soon as I finish this bottle."

"I'm only joking, Matt. You stay with the ladies, and I'll do all the hard work. Don't worry about me."

Matt laughed and smiled over at Lisa. She thought how nice it was here with him and all the family. Perhaps they could wander along the beach later, with a glass of wine, and sit on the rocks and chat as they had that first day when she arrived back in Cove Bay and felt devastated by the news that Peter was single and eager to get back with her. How long ago that seemed now. And how wonderful that she hadn't bumped into Peter since that ridiculous night at the sports bar. He'd tried to arrange to meet her loads of times and continued to call and text, but he'd got the message that she wasn't interested. And she knew he wouldn't come to work to find her because Nancy would kick him out.

"I'm going to get a refill," she said. "Anybody else interested?"

"I'd love one," said Matt. "But unlike you ladies of leisure over here, I've got work to do at the barbeque station. I can't sit around here wasting time."

He got up to head back over to her dad, kissing Lisa lightly on the cheek as he went past.

They sat and drank wine on the beach until late that night, watching the sea roll up the sand and enjoying how the moonlit waves made the water shimmer and dance. Misty radiance lit up the sky all around them.

"I should go,' said Matt, not moving at all. 'Game day tomorrow."

"Have you got much preparation to do?"

"I've got loads to sort out, but I want to stay with you. Make me go."

"That's difficult to do when I want you to stay."

"I'll stay then. We'll lie here all night and look at the moon."

"It's probably going to get cold soon, though. And it's not going to be very comfortable lying on the damp sand."

"Yeah, there is that. I suppose I should make a move."

Matt sat up, and Lisa followed suit.

"I've had a lovely evening," he said.

"Me too."

He leaned over and kissed her, then moved his head back and looked deep into her eyes.

"You are adorable, Ms Lopez. Very lovely indeed."

Lisa took his hand and kissed it. "You too, Mr Matt Rowls. You, too."

They walked together to Matt's car, holding hands, occasionally glancing at one another, like a couple falling in love.

"Do you know how soppy you have made me?" Matt asked.

"No. Do tell me."

"The guys keep mocking me at work because I look like I'm in a dream half the time, then when I got a new phone yesterday. I had to put in a temporary password, so I put 'LisaLopez1.' How sad is that?"

"Pretty damn sad," she agreed, as he put her arms around her.

"Don't tell anyone. It's our secret," he said, kissing her on the top of her head and preparing to get into the car. "Fancy breakfast tomorrow?"

"Urghh...I can't," she replied. "I've agreed to go shopping in Plymouth with the girls. I'm thinking of a million ways to escape it, but they are all quite determined."

"That'll be fun," said Matt. "Your sisters are great."

"My sisters are lovely; it's the shopping I'm not looking forward to. I find it so boring."

"If you can escape it, come and have breakfast with me. I'm going to the Flip Flop Bar at 10 am for their match day special breakfast. If you fancy it, text me. I'll come and pick you up."

"I'm surprised they'll let you in there. Didn't the arrival of the Sharks and the new rugby club bar kill off all their business?"

"Yes, it did a bit; that's why I feel I ought to go down there. I'm signing some programmes for them and giving a small talk about the club and the players. Come with me?"

"I'll text you if I can get out of this shopping trip."

Lisa should have known better. There was no way on God's earth she was getting out of the clothes extravaganza that her sisters had planned for her.

"You promised," said Isabella. "Come on; we're going to have a brilliant time. We're meeting Sophia in Cove Bay for lunch at Cafe Deli; then we're off to the big city for shopping."

"Oh, God."

THE NEXT MORNING, her sisters were up and planning their day out.

"Up and at 'em...rise and shine," shouted Emma.

"Yes, yes, yes, I'm coming," said Lisa. "Just give me a minute to have a shower."

"You can take all the minutes you like, but we're leaving here with you at 11m, even if we have to carry you out in your pyjamas.

"I don't understand you lot; what is the attraction of shopping all the time? We could go out and have fun somewhere."

"We'll have lots of fun shopping, just you see."

Lisa hated the crowds, the queueing, and the process of taking off one set of clothes to try on another. And, to top it all, she wasn't any good at shopping. She didn't have the gene that her sisters had. Emma wasn't particularly interested in anything to do with her looks either, but the other two were complete style icons compared to Lisa.

When she went shopping with Isabella and Sophia, the two of them would drape garments around themselves. They would adorn themselves with accessories, jumpers and skirts and look fantastic. Lisa would stand there with her arms folded, not understanding what was happening. In the same way that she could spend an hour and a half watching a rugby game and not understand who was doing what to whom and why they were doing it, she could also stand in a clothes shop for an hour and a half trying lots of clothes on and not understand which were better and why.

By 11 am, the pressure to leave was on. "Chop, chop," said Isabella. "We're meeting Sophia on her lunch break for a bite to eat; then we're hitting Plymouth."

"Why don't you go and meet Soph without me? You know how much I hate walking around shops. You'll have a much better time without me moaning all day."

"Nope. You are coming, whether you like it or not."

"OK, OK," she said. She knew when she was beaten.

. . .

THE SISTERS SAT in Cafe Deli at lunchtime, surrounded by the residue of the meal they'd enjoyed. They had been joined by Angie Ball, the beautiful manageress of the restaurant, and the group of women were catching up on local gossip.

'Quite honestly, I would take home all of those players if I were a few years younger,' said Angie, tossing back her blonde hair and smiling seductively through expertly applied makeup. Angie was in her late 50s, though no one was entirely sure of her age. It was information that she kept hidden from even her closest friends. 'I'd certainly make room for that team coach. What's his name?'

"Matt?" said Sophia, looking directly at Lisa.

Lisa felt herself turning scarlet.

'That's right. He's very hunky. I'll have to wait until James goes away for the weekend, then pounce on him."

"I'm not sure you're allowed to go pouncing on your men. There's a law against behaviour like that," said Isabella. "Anyway, he might have a girlfriend or something."

Lisa felt herself colour even further as Isabella smiled at her.

"I'm not bothered whether he has a girlfriend or not. I have a boyfriend, remember."

Angie's (considerably younger) boyfriend was James, a gorgeous 35-year-old with whom Sophia had once shared a few dates many years previously. He worked in the cafe with Angie, doing all of the work, as far as the girls could see, while Angie chatted, flirted and planned her trips to the beautician.

"Anyway, what are you ladies up to today?"

"We're going shopping in Plymouth to buy Lisa lots of new clothes, and I am looking forward to it, even if she is not," said Isabella. "She's lost so much weight her clothes are hanging off her. Except she hasn't lost weight on her breasts, of course, so her figure looks amazing. She's such a cow. Anyway, we're going to buy her some drop-dead gorgeous outfits."

"I noticed you'd lost weight, darling. You look fabulous. I hope Peter sees you and realises what a fool he's been. That man needs a slap. Now, I should be off. You girls have a wonderful time, and I'll see you soon."

"Thanks, Angie," said Lisa, as Angie air-kissed her goodbyes and headed over to join James.

"Well, you need to keep an eye on Matt," said Isabella. "Angie is definitely keen. You don't want her to get her claws into your boyfriend."

"He's not my boyfriend. We're just getting to know one another."

"He's your boyfriend," said Emma. "Definitely. No doubt about it."

"Of course he is," said Isabella. "He's your boyfriend, and you should be very happy about it. He's bloody gorgeous and lovely."

"I know he's gorgeous and lovely, and I like him. But he's not my boyfriend," said Lisa. Despite how much she liked him, she was desperate not to get too involved too quickly.

"OK. We'll take your word for that. Now is everyone ready for shopping?" said Emma.

"I'm going to need a glass of wine before we go," said Lisa, signalling to Angie, who immediately clicked her jewel-clad fingers, and James rushed over to take their order.

"I need a relationship like that," said Isabella as James came bounding up to them.

"A glass of the New Zealand Sauvignon," said Lisa. "I'm being tortured this afternoon, so make it a big one."

"A large one coming up," he said, smiling warmly at the sisters as he walked away. A glass of wine later, Lisa could delay things no longer. "Why don't we get a bottle?" she tried, but Isabella was having none of it.

"Car. You. Now. We're going to Plymouth."

The traffic en route to the city was much better than Lisa had feared, and they were there in under half an hour, but the crowds when they got there were terrible. They hit the busy High Street, determined to buy Lisa some clothes that fit and that didn't hang off her like everything else in her wardrobe, while crowds packed the streets and shops.

"We need to go to Gap first," said Sophia. "We need to get you some jeans. I know how much you love jeans."

Lisa breathed a sigh of relief. When they'd talked about clothes shopping, she thought she'd be carted around all the posh shops and urged to buy little dresses and high-heel sandals. Going into Gap for jeans was much more her sort of thing.

"We are going to buy you clothes that you can actually wear and enjoy wearing but also look good," said Sophia. "I've taken the afternoon off work, so we are going to get you the best wardrobe we can in the time we have. OK?"

"OK," said Lisa obediently.

She followed Sophia around like a little puppy, weaving in and out of the racks while her sister picked up clothes she thought would be suitable. "Right—boyfriend jeans—you need these," she said. "We also want some skinny jeans, and I think some cropped white jeans would look good." She called over the assistant, and the two talked together, looking over at Lisa before the lady went off and came back with armfuls of clothes.

"Right, follow me," said Sophia.

Much to Lisa's surprise, it turned out that jeans came in all sorts of different shapes and sizes. The boyfriend jeans that Sophia had been so keen on her having were lovely—quite loose-fitting and comfortable, as well as looking good. "You know your stuff, don't you, Sophia?" she said.

"This is coming as a surprise to you?" said Sophia sarcastically, rubbing Lisa's shoulder as she surveyed the clothing on her.

"Try these white jeans on. I know you won't like them because they are tight-fitting, but they will allow you to wear lots of the tops in your wardrobe that are loose now—and make them look stylish. You can also wear them with either flats or with high heels."

Lisa knew she would wear them with flats—most likely with her Converses.

With everything she tried on, she emerged from the changing room to comments, prodding and—on a couple of occasions—a round of applause from her sisters. They were causing a commotion in the shop, but it didn't seem to matter. Sophia had this effect on everyone; everywhere she went...people would stop, look and admire her. Lisa knew she was only being given all this attention because she was in her older sister's wake. It was a familiar feeling. She had gone through school as the younger sister of the very beautiful Sophia, who everyone wanted to know. Beautiful people have a different life than the rest of us, thought Lisa. It was just lovely that Sophia was in hers.

"Will you try those skinny jeans on with this white shirt?" asked Sophia, handing a soft white shirt over to Lisa.

"OK," said Lisa, disappearing back into the changing room.

She put the white shirt on and tucked it into the jeans, slipping on a pair of high-heel boots that Isabella had lent her. She looked in the mirror and, even though she felt uncomfortable and a bit tarty, she knew she looked good. She walked out of the changing room, spinning around in front of her audience.

"You look wonderful," said a male voice. She looked up, and right in front of her, staring straight at her, was Peter.

"Don't look surprised, sweetheart; you do. You look amazing."

"Just get out of here," said Emma. "Can't you leave her alone? Don't you know what you did to her? You're trying to ruin her life. If you think you can come simpering back into it with a few compliments... just get out of here."

"Go on, Peter," said Sophia. "We made it very clear to you how she feels; if you don't go away, I'll get the store manager to throw you out."

"What on earth am I supposed to have done wrong?" asked Peter. "I was just going to see whether Lisa wanted to...."

But he never finished his sentence. Sophia had summoned help with a click of her elegant fingers, and he was bundled out of the shop while Lisa returned to the security, comfort and safety of a small, wooden changing room in a large branch of Gap. She pulled off the jeans, removed the shirt, kicked off the boots, and climbed into her old clothes. All she wanted to do now was be at home, sitting in her bedroom, on the veranda, looking out over the beach and into the beautiful, blue sea beyond it—a place where she felt safe and happy.

"You OK in there?" asked Emma.

"Yes, I'm fine," Lisa replied. "I could've done without him turning up. For the first time in my life, I was enjoying this clothes shopping nonsense."

"Well, he's gone now. We can carry on," said Emma.

"You know what? I want to go home."

"Just a couple more shops? It would be a real shame if you let him ruin your day. He's not worth it, Lise, honestly."

"No, I'll buy these clothes, but I don't want to shop anymore; I just want to be at home. Please? Why don't we get a bottle of wine and have a good chat at home, or go to a local bar or something? I don't want to walk around this place for the rest of the afternoon, dreading seeing him wherever I go."

"OK," said Emma. "Are you sure, though? Can't you just forget about Peter? You look better than you ever have in your life before; you've got a super-fantastic new boyfriend who thinks the world of you and a job you love. Don't let that dickhead ruin everything."

"He won't ruin everything, but it's not as simple and easy as you're making out. I just want to go home. If it's a problem, I'll get a cab."

"It's not a problem. Listen, I'll sort the others out. You gather those clothes up, buy them, and let's get you home."

Lisa didn't know whether her sisters understood why she found it so difficult to see Peter. Sophia would tell her later that she would've been delighted to have bumped into an ex when looking so good.

"It's the dream. You will bump into your ex at some point and want it to be when you're all dressed up and looking fantastic. You pulled it off, sister! First, you're in a red evening dress; then you're in skin-tight jeans that show off your amazing figure."

But Lisa didn't feel like that. She knew that Sophia meant well but clearly didn't understand what Peter had put Lisa through. Not that Lisa could blame her. Perhaps you had to have had your life turned upside down and smashed against the rocks to understand why it was hard. Perhaps all the dreams you had for yourself had to be thrown into the sea and washed away by giant waves before you understood what heartbreak and misery were.

She sometimes felt like no one understood. Lisa had always been calm, rational and easy-going, but the breakup with Peter had wounded something deep inside her. The sight of him just now had brought back all the horrors of the past - the way in which he had taken away her trust, her joie de vivre and her dignity. He'd also taken away the future they had planned, the love she thought they shared. She'd felt cast adrift by the one person she thought was there to provide a safe haven.

She was delighted that she'd met Matt and knew what an excellent 'catch' he was but seeing Peter had reminded her that she was still vulnerable and that it might take time for her to trust a man again.

CHAPTER 11

"What if they don't like me?" asked Lisa.

"They will." Matt squeezed Lisa's thigh as they drove along the seafront, then into the countryside, heading for Hope Bay, to the west of Cove Bay, where Matt's parents were waiting to greet them.

"They might think I'm not good enough for you," she said. "They probably expect you to be shacking up with a gorgeous cheerleader."

"They will be delighted that I'm not shacking up with a cheer-leader," said Matt, laughing at Lisa. "Do you have no self-confidence at all?"

"Not a great deal," she replied. "Perhaps they'll hate me for that?"

Matt laughed. "You are lovely," he said. "Really lovely. I "adore you, and so will they."

"Well, I'm glad you think so." She had her doubts, though. Emma had met Matt's parents several times and described them as posh, cold and humourless. 'The opposite of Matt,' Emma had said. 'Honestly, they're not at all like him. He left them with me at the bar, and I didn't know what to say to them.'

Lisa was wearing the white jeans that Sophia had insisted she buy. She had worn the jeans many times, and they always looked great.

Sophia knew what she was doing. They were as comfortable as denim jeans, but the fact that they were white made them look so dressy. On top, she had a green chiffon flowing blouse she borrowed from Isabella and some kitten-heeled shoes. Not bad for a scruffy old gardener.

"It's here, just around this corner," said Matt, turning the wheel sharply and taking them up along the path toward a big house.

"Oh my goodness, look at this..." said Lisa. "Wow, look at those gardens. Is this your parents' house? It's incredible." It seemed odd that his parents would have such a beautiful house when he lived in a tiny, one-bedroom apartment, but Lisa thought it best not to mention that; it was none of her business.

"Can we go and look at the gardens later?" she asked. "Some of these shrubs and trees are so mature...it's beautiful."

"My dad is going to love you. He is going to adore you. Anyone interested in gardens always delights him. The fact that you're lovely and pretty as well will knock him sideways. He is going to be in his element."

The house was enormous. It must have been three times the size of the house that Lisa had grown up in. She had never seen anything quite like it. It reminded her of *Downton Abbey*. In some ways, it was like Suffolk Manor, but grander. Matt must think her parents' home was scruffy compared to this.

"Ready?" asked Matt. He opened the car door and climbed out, coming around to open the door for Lisa in his traditional, gentle-manly manner.

"Watch out, here come the dogs," he said. Three large, red setters circled them, barking and sniffing—seemingly delighted that one of their masters had returned.

"Sit," shouted Matt, and the dogs sat instantly, looking up at him for approval.

"OK, let's go."

Lisa was terrified. She wasn't dressed right. Why had she worn white jeans? A couple of minutes ago, she'd felt great, but now she felt entirely out of place. Her "kitten-heel" shoes would make one step in the garden difficult; the white jeans would be filthy in five seconds flat if she started playing with the dogs, and the green chiffon top felt more like beach wear than appropriate to meet Matt's mum and dad. She should have worn jeans and boots.

Then she saw Matt's mom.

"Hello, my dear, how nice to meet you. I'm Christie." She was beautiful, and Lisa did not think she was being unkind by assuming that the woman had had a lot of surgery! Her taut face was largely unlined and made up to perfection, and she had long, blonde hair cascading around her shoulders. She embraced Lisa in a rather unaffectionate hug before leading her into the house.

"Matt, bring the bags in here, dear."

"We're not staying," he said. "Lisa's got work tomorrow, and I'm meeting investors."

"Oh no, that's such a shame, dear. Are you not going to stay? It seems a shame to drive."

"It's only about 20 minutes," said Matt.

"I know, darling, but it means you can't have a drink with lunch."

"I promise we'll come again soon. I don't think I'll be able to keep Lisa away. She looked at the garden as we drove through and was hooked for life."

"Goodness, do you enjoy the outdoors? I'm afraid I find it tiresome," she said. "But if you want to go out and take a look, there are spare boots in the back." Phew, at least that was one less thing to worry about.

Matt's parents were lovely. His mom was rather cold and difficult to know at first. All she wanted to talk about was the redecoration of the house she was engaged in, and Lisa felt she had nothing to contribute on that front. Luckily, Matt's dad and his younger brother, Freddie, more than made up for it and were warm and chatty, just like Matt.

"What did your parents do?" she asked Matt as he took her on a tour of the place. What she meant was, "how in the hell did they make so much money that they could afford an astonishing place like this?" But she didn't want to be quite that obvious.

"My dad used to be a doctor," Matt said.

Lisa was impressed. It was a very important and valuable job, but would that income pay for this incredible place?

"Mom never worked; she was a social butterfly when we were younger...always organising parties and dinners. The house was never empty. When I was growing up, we had a team of eight gardeners working, as well as staff in the house. Mum used to marshal them and ensure everything was exactly how she wanted it to be. She can be quite a formidable woman, my mother."

Lisa didn't doubt that for a second, but she had become even more intrigued about how they managed to fund this lavish lifestyle.

Perhaps his dad used to be a super-successful Hollywood cosmetic surgeon or something? How else could he make millions from being a doctor?

Lunch in the house was called soon after they arrived, with the ringing of a bell. Matt grimaced when he heard the ringing. "That's such an awful affectation. I wish they'd get rid of it; there are only two of them here most of the time; they don't need a bell ringer to tell them when their meals are ready."

"If you want to use the powder room before sitting down, it's just through the library," Christie said. Lisa smiled and said that she was fine; no powder was needed. But she knew she needed to remember that quote to tell the girls. 'The powder room is just through the library.' Emma would love that.

CHRISTIE JOINED them at the table, leaving Lisa wondering who would bring the food. Perhaps it was self-service, but she couldn't see any food bowls anywhere.

She looked over at Matt, hopeful of an explanation. Within minutes, an answer was forthcoming. The doors swung open, and two maids walked in, both dressed in black. They carried trays of food and walked the length of the long table, placing small plates in front of everyone.

"Please start," said the lady of the house.

"This looks delicious," said Matt, examining his lobster.

"Lovely, thank you," Lisa said.

"How are things going with the team, Matt? Is everything OK? Do you think it's going to make a lot of money?"

"Good. A 100% record so far, mum. It's early days, but they're looking good."

"Great. And financially?"

"Early days, mum."

"And you're in that little flat for the time being?"

"Yes, mum."

The starters were followed by chicken with asparagus, which tasted so fresh and delicious it was as if it melted in her mouth. The atmosphere was warm and convivial, but the conversation barely touched the surface. They asked no questions about her at all, which felt very strange. Matt offered lots of information and told them about Lisa's love of gardening, but they seemed to have no follow-up questions. All they seemed interested in was how much money the club was making and when Matt would be moving house. When Lisa asked about the house move and said she wasn't aware that he was moving, they apologised and fell into a deep silence.

"Have you taken many girls home before?" Lisa asked as they drove back at the end of the evening, both of them pink-cheeked from their bracing walk in the countryside.

"Not many," he said. It seemed a bit vague.

"Not many?" she asked. "Some, then."

"Why do you want to know?"

"Because I don't feel I know anything about your past relation-ships," she said. "You know everything about mine."

"OK, none," he said. "You are the first girl I've taken back there because I really like you and want you to be in my life. OK?"

"OK," she said. "Are you moving soon?"

"Mum gets a bit ahead of herself. I will be moving, but not quite yet."

"I don't think they liked me," Lisa concluded. "I knew they wouldn't."

"They loved you," said Matt. "Trust me, you'd know about it if they didn't like you. They're just not used to meeting girlfriends."

Perhaps that's all it was...the lunch had felt a little awkward because it was the first time Matt had ever taken a girlfriend back. But why hadn't he taken anyone before? Something felt as if it wasn't quite right. The problem was, she didn't know what.

CHAPTER 12

$\mathcal{I}$n the following weeks, the countdown to the Spring Ball began, Lisa organised the preparation of the garden as if she were organising a military invasion.

All her staff were gathered around her, as well as Nancy, sipping rather elegantly on a cup of coffee in the most delicate china. Lisa looked over at her - she was a beautiful woman with delicate features and a beautiful, elegant profile. Her thick white blonde hair was caught in a tortoiseshell clip at the nape of her slender neck. She had a very different sort of beauty to Angie's blousy look or Christie's wind-tunnel-like appearance. Nancy had wrinkles, but they didn't detract from her loveliness. Angie covered hers with makeup, and Christie had sand-blasted hers away.

"We must ensure that the four areas are as immaculate as possible," said Lisa. "Does anyone need reminding about the four areas?"

There was a chortle of laughter from the staff. They got her joke: she'd talked about nothing but the four areas since her return to Suffolk Manor months ago. She had wanted to keep it all as simple and logical as possible and to ensure that each garden area was tended to. This seemed like the best way.

It wasn't rocket science, but she found it worked better if you divided up a big job into small, manageable parts that people could relate to. All the gardeners would then be given a clear area to work in and precise tasks to do; it was Lisa's job to ensure that this all added up to an immaculate, stunning garden in time for the Spring Ball.

Area One was the section closest to the front of the house—the places guests would see most closely. Area Two contained the gardens that guests were likely to wander around and congregate in—the rose garden, particularly, but also the wind chime garden, the south garden, and the Lady Mary garden. They all had to look great. The Lady Mary garden had all sorts of little places for children to play— and Nancy had been adamant that children should be invited to the Spring Ball and be allowed to have lots of fun, so there needed to be areas for them which looked great and were completely safe. There was going to be a treasure hunt held in the garden, and Lisa knew that it needed to be completely safe and devoid of anything prickly, stingy or thorny for Nancy to be happy.

Area Three was the large lawn at the back of the property where guests would go out for drinks—and to where they would spill in between dancing and chatting. Area Four was the rest of the estate— the more out-of-reach places people would be unlikely to wander to but still needed to be safe and look as lovely as possible.

Barry, her big tough worker who'd joined them from Germany, would be doing all the heavy lifting and complex machinery work. She would send Dan with him for the day. "Can you look at Area Four today? Just ensure that there aren't any branches down from trees or any horror that we need to be aware of. I'd like you to start at Area Four and work in."

She assigned areas—and specific responsibilities within the areas —to all her staff, ensuring that every little detail was properly covered.

"I'm going to go with Mandy and James to the Lady Mary garden this morning, so if anyone wants me, that's where I will be. I have my phone on me, so call if there are any problems, and I'll come and help.

Assuming there are no problems, I'll see you all back in the conservatory at lunchtime so we can have a debrief and work out what the biggest areas of concern are. Is that OK?"

The staff headed off on their various tasks while Lisa wandered over to talk to Nancy. "Everything OK?" she asked.

"Everything is perfect," said Nancy. "I'm not sure what we would've done if you hadn't come back."

"I'm sure you'd have coped," said Lisa. "But it is very lovely to be back."

"It's lovely to have you back," said Nancy, giving Lisa a huge hug and spilling half of her coffee onto the terrace before admonishing herself. "I'm so clumsy," she said. "I'll see you at lunchtime, OK?"

THE MORNING WENT past in a blur of digging, weeding, pruning and looking around to ensure that there were no rough edges, sharp corners or prickly plants that would injure little hands when they played their treasure hunt.

At lunchtime, she went around and talked to all the gardeners, making a list of where the potential problems were. To be honest, there were very few. There was a concern about the perimeter fence and a slight issue with the stables at the back of the field—one of the slats had come down at the side of it—but nothing drastic; these things were easily mended. She arranged for a handyperson to come out as soon as possible. She was feeling more and more confident that this was going to be the best Spring Ball ever.

In the afternoon, she worked alone along the main pathway leading to the house where everyone coming to the ball would travel. For some of them, it would be their first sight of the house; for all of them, it would be their first impression of this year's gardens, so Lisa wanted it to look immaculate.

The plants she'd carefully tended bloomed beautifully, precisely as Lisa had planned. She stood up, stretching her legs and arms and breathing in the soft, fresh spring air. She could feel the sun on her skin. This was why she loved her job—working where she could breathe fresh air and feel full of goodness, life and vitality. As she brought her gaze down from the skies, she saw what looked like Matt's car pulling into the parking area just next to the rose garden. No, it couldn't be. She was starting to go mad—visualising him appearing all over the place, like an oasis in the desert. She took a couple of gulps of her water and splashed a little onto her face, lifting her eyes to the skies again to let the sun dry the water. When she brought her head down, she saw a familiar figure walking up the pathway; it was Matt. What on earth was Matt doing here? She stood with hands on her hips, waiting for him to reach her.

"You look like the security officer standing there," he said. "Are you going to let me pass?"

"Only if you tell me what your business is."

"I need to have a quick chat with Nancy; then, I'll be back to talk to you... I have a proposal for you," he said.

"OK, in that case, you can pass," said Lisa. "To be honest, I let all the good-looking men in, so don't go thinking you're special or anything."

"Ha. See you in about thirty minutes," he said.

Lisa smiled. She wondered what on earth he was going to talk to Nancy about. It was the second time she had seen him at the house. This wasn't the sort of place people just popped into, and Nancy wasn't the sort of woman to whom you paid social calls. She wasn't like that. Her days were filled with meetings and charities, foundations, balls and events. What was Matt seeing her about?

Lisa continued gardening, moving slowly toward the house before sitting on the steps outside the main door, drinking water and surveying all her hard work.

"It's looking great," said Matt, sitting beside her. "You're good at this gardening business, aren't you?"

"I like to think so," said Lisa as Matt pulled her closer to him, wrapping his arm around her shoulder and kissing her tenderly.

"You taste like gardens in springtime," he said, holding her head in his hands and looking deeply into her eyes. "You taste very nice. I might do that again.

Before Lisa could object, Matt kissed her again—more passionately this time—pulling her towards him and letting his hands move gently inside her blouse, over her shoulders, so his hands caressed her bra straps as his kisses became more intense. Lisa pulled back.

"Everything OK?"

"Yes," she said, surprising herself. Her head was telling her to push him away and storm off; her heart, and every other part of her, wanted him to kiss her forever.

"This isn't the best place for this," she avoided his eyes as she spoke.

"Come with me," he said, taking her hand and leading her to the other side of the house and down into the rose garden. They got there to see lots of gardeners busy tending to the flowers.

"It's no good—I've got people working everywhere," she said. Her immaculate planning meant people were working all over the land.

"I want you," he said, leaning closely into her. "Come with me."

It was so unlike her, so unlike anything she'd done before, but, in her rain boots and with mud on her face and sweat in her hair, Lisa followed behind Matt as he led her to his car. The sexual tension between them built as they sped along the narrow lanes towards Kingsbridge was palpable. She had no idea where they were going, but she didn't care; she just wanted to be alone with this man.

Matt pulled into The George Hotel—the most beautiful place in the area. It looked expensive. Could she go in there like this?

"I look a mess," she said.

"You look gorgeous," he replied. His voice seemed deeper, and in his eyes, there was a longing she didn't remember ever seeing before. "Don't worry about anything."

As they walked into the hotel, hand in hand, with no cases, looking more like they had come to work on the plumbing than to enjoy the exclusive facilities, Matt walked confidently to the desk.

"A double room, please," he said. And that was that.

They walked slowly toward the elevator, not speaking. Why weren't they talking? Was his heart racing like hers was?

The room was enormous; a great big bed, a lovely sofa, a small writing desk, and stunning views across the hills. Lisa looked out at the trees and lawns leading towards the hills, disappearing into the distance.

"It's lovely," she said, her voice croaking with emotion.

"You're lovely," he replied, kissing her. His arms slid around her back, and he pulled her towards him and kissed her. She felt a wave of desire crash through her. Still kissing her, he moved his hands to the buttons on her shirt.

"God, you're beautiful," he said.

She knew she wasn't beautiful; Sophia was beautiful, with her perfect button nose and sense of style; film stars were beautiful. She wasn't, but at this moment, she felt like she was. She felt like the most beautiful woman in the world.

Lisa watched Matt's big hands struggle with the little buttons until he pulled her shirt off, moaning as he saw her standing there in just her bra. How she wished she was wearing something more alluring than a sports bra. She looked at him, looking at her, and it might have been the most exciting thing she'd ever seen. The only parts of her body she felt confident about were her breasts; they were large but still perky. But - really - the extra-strength sports bra wasn't doing her any favours. She reached around and undid it, letting her large breasts bounce free, watching his face all the time.

"God, you're gorgeous," he said, stroking them and cupping them as he kissed her. He pushed his tongue deep into her mouth. There was something so sexy about his roughness—not like Peter at all; Peter had always been so smooth, his skin so well-cared-for. Matt was different. He pulled down her shorts and tore off her underwear as she reached out to touch him, feeling him through his denim jeans. She wanted him inside her so much she could hardly breathe with excitement at the thought of it. She kicked off her clothes that hovered down by the ankles, forcing them over her boots as he removed the rest of his clothes.

"I want to make love to you," he said.

Lisa was still on the pill. She hadn't come off it after her relationship with Peter collapsed. "I want to, too," she said, and he entered her slowly, looking at her so tenderly as she watched him—the veins on his neck standing up, the look of ecstasy on his face, the dark stubble on his chin, the thick hair on his chest, and the way the muscles in his arms stood out. God, it felt good. Everything outside of them disappeared as they moved together. Lisa felt her feelings mount. She was going to have an orgasm. It had been so long. She wanted this feeling to last forever. Matt began to moan; it was getting closer. Lisa relaxed and let the feelings flood over her. God, this felt good.

"I love you," said Matt. "I love you."

THEY LAY THERE AFTERWARDS, their legs all tangled together, Lisa's hair all over the place, Matt smiling—content and happy.

He looked up and smiled. Then he began to laugh.

"What is it?" she asked.

"Nothing," he said. "I suppose it's the first time I've ever made love to a woman in a pair of wellington boots."

Lisa looked down and smiled at him. "I must be the unsexiest person on the planet," she said.

"Well, it's certainly an unusual look," said Matt. "But definitely NOT unsexy."

LISA LAUGHED and ruffled his hair affectionately. "Blimey, I should go," she said, looking at her watch.

"Why? Let's stay here and get room service. I think they've got a swimming pool downstairs and a spa. Let's have the best afternoon and evening ever."

"What about work?" said Lisa. "I left without even mentioning to Nancy that I was going. I can't run out on the poor woman again. I need to go back and finish off those roses."

"I talked to Nancy. I told her I was whisking you away; she knows exactly where you are," said Matt.

"And she didn't mind?" asked Lisa.

"Nope. In fact, she thought it was a rather good idea," said Matt. "She probably didn't realise exactly what I was going to do to you, but she thought it was a lovely idea that I wanted to take you out for the afternoon. I told her I'd get you back there for tomorrow morning."

"Well," said Lisa. "Well, that's all rather wonderful, isn't it?"

CHAPTER 13

*L*isa woke up slowly, stretching out, feline-fashion, before feeling the hard wooden floor beneath her. Where was she? She sat up and looked around: Oh, the hotel. Matt was standing by the open window at the far side of the room; the light gauze that hung behind the curtains floated in the early evening breeze as he tapped away at his phone, oblivious to the fact that he was being watched.

Lisa felt a knot tighten in her stomach. "Who are you texting?" she asked. Matt jumped as she spoke. He hadn't realized she was awake. He turned around to look at her.

"No one," he said, pushing his phone under the cushion on the large wingback chair next to him and walking towards her.

Why had he done that with his phone? That's the way Peter used to behave with his phone.

"You do look rather fetching like that," he said.

Lisa looked down. She was still naked except for her wellington boots. "Yep, I think it's probably time I removed these," she said. "Who were you texting?"

Matt leaned over and pulled the boot off, removing her socks and gently massaging her feet. He didn't speak.

"Who were you texting?" she repeated. "Is everything OK?"

"Everything's wonderful," he said. "Stop worrying. I wonder how big the bath is in there."

"I'm sure the bath is plenty big enough for two," she said, smiling at him. It was a slightly uncomfortable smile. It seemed odd that he wouldn't answer her questions about who he was texting. Matt smiled at the thought of their bath together, raising his eyebrows in happy anticipation and walked into the bathroom. Lisa watched him go.

"Was everything OK?" she asked. "I mean…with the texts."

Matt kept walking. "Yes, everything's perfect." He had very broad shoulders and quite a thick waist. She imagined that when he was at his athletic best, he'd have had one of those triangle shapes that great athletes have, with the wide shoulders disappearing into a small, toned waist. But she liked him like this, a big rectangle walking around the place.

He also had very large thighs. She didn't think she'd ever seen a man with such large thighs. He walked into the bathroom and then reappeared with a smile. "The bath is plenty big enough," he said. "And it's one of those Jacuzzis. I'll see if there's any champagne in the minibar."

Lisa laid back on the floor as the sounds of water gushing into the bath drifted in from the bathroom, and she heard Matt fiddling with the fridge. This was lovely. So lovely. She just needed to stop thinking about the texts he was sending. It must be work. He probably didn't want to bore her with the details of match tactics and team selection. She couldn't compare him to Peter. That wouldn't be fair. But a small part of her, just a flicker of her, was concerned.

She looked up to see Matt standing next to her with two glasses of champagne, completely naked and looking at her with such warmth. "You look miles away," he said. "I think our bath is ready."

Lisa walked toward him, wrapping her arms around him and hugging him tightly. Surely Matt wouldn't do what Peter had done? Surely this was different.

She sunk under the water and looked over at him as he climbed in, clicking the button to send the bubbles surging up all around them.

She must try to keep all this in perspective. He was lovely; he said he loved her. Peter arranging to see his lover by text was different from this. Matt was different.

But, as she sipped champagne in the perfect bathroom of the perfect hotel room with the perfect man, her head was in turmoil. There were all those cheerleaders around him all the time...they were so beautiful and SO available. And what about the fans? They'd love to bag a night with him. Was he sleeping with them? As Matt massaged her feet and looked at her lovingly, she knew exactly what she needed to do. She had to check his phone; she wouldn't be able to relax until she knew who he'd been texting right after they had made love.

CHAPTER 14

*I*t was early Saturday morning. Matt strode around the ground, looking up at the stands and around the outfield. He had never taken time to congratulate himself on what he'd achieved here, but this morning, in an empty stadium before the crowds arrived for the biggest game of the season, he smiled. It had all gone so well; financially backing twenty-five per cent of the project himself had been a considerable risk, but it was paying off. He'd end up rich. Money wasn't a great motivator for him, but he knew his mum would be delighted. She'd thought so little of him when he first started playing rugby, then so much of him when the huge money contracts poured in. Even prouder again when he'd invested it all into the property scene and made millions. Now, he was about to become even richer and make her prouder. It was all his mum seemed to care about. But he loved her and wanted her to be proud of him.

To him, plenty of things were way more important than money. For example, the friendship group he'd found here in Cove Bay. Emma was a little superstar as bar manager, making sure the staff were happy and that there was a lovely atmosphere in the place, even for those not interested in the sport. Emma would keep them drinking and partying, and the turnover would continue to grow. And eventually, profits would start to appear...big profits that he could invest locally in the youth in this area and use to buy his dream home and create a great life for himself.

Matt was looking forward to moving out of the little apartment he'd rented. He was too old to be bedding down in a one-bedroom place that was too run down to invite anyone to visit, but he wasn't much of a homemaker and had just grabbed the first place he saw while organising the buying of his dream house.

Now he longed to take his belongings out of storage, move in properly and settle in the area. He wanted a place where Lisa could come to, and they could spend more time alone and get to know one another. It was hard at the moment. Lisa's family was lovely. He adored her mom and dad; they'd been the first people he'd met when he came to the area—such kind, genuine, warm and sincere people. He thought a lot of them.

The only thing he was confused about was Lisa's reaction to him after their afternoon and evening together at the hotel. Since then, they hadn't been able to spend time together; she was always so busy preparing for the Spring Ball. He understood and loved her commitment to it; he just hoped he hadn't spooked her by taking their relationship to the next level. Perhaps telling her that he loved her was too much? Something had turned her away from him, and he didn't like it.

He looked at his watch. He had time to pop over to the house now. He would try and persuade Lisa to come to the game today.

LISA FINISHED WASHING the dishes and handing them to her mum to dry. "I think that's it," she said. "Anything else need doing?"

"No, that's everything. Thanks, Lisa."

"I think I'll go and have a bath, then." Lisa washed out the dishcloth and hung it over the edge of the sink to dry.

"Are you going to the game today?" asked her mom.

"No, I don't think I will."

"Really? I thought you might want to be there for Matt. It's a big game today. We are all going," she said.

"Yes, I know."

"Are you sure everything is OK," asked her mum. "Everything OK with you and Matt? You've been very quiet recently and haven't seen him for a few days."

"Yes, everything is fine. Honestly, Mom, don't worry. I want to spend the afternoon doing a few bits and pieces in the house."

Lisa left the room and wandered to her bedroom, gathering her things together and heading off to the bathroom to run herself a bath. The truth was that she was worried about Matt and didn't know how to handle it. She'd backed away after their time together in the hotel not because it was all too much - strangely, it wasn't. And she certainly hadn't gone off Matt. Quite the opposite. She liked him, and seeing him texting and refusing to say who he'd been texting had made her worried. What did she know about Matt?

Peter had hurt her, and she didn't want the same thing to happen again. It was all so frustrating. Why wouldn't he tell her who he was sending messages to? It wasn't right. She couldn't relax with a man and have a proper relationship with him if he was hiding things from her. She'd kept away from him ever since and pretended that she was too busy at work.

Lisa had just relaxed into the bubbles when she heard the doorbell ring. Her mum's familiar pit-patting footsteps moved toward the front door; then, she heard a voice she recognised.

"Matt's here," shouted her mum.

Lisa felt a little flutter of excitement. Despite her fears about him, she still liked him a lot. She stepped out of the water, dried herself and dashed into her bedroom. After towel-drying her hair, she applied a light, tinted moisturiser to her skin. Then she slipped on a pair of simple jeans and a white T-shirt and headed out to find Matt and her mom.

The two of them had taken their coffees out onto the beach; Lisa could see them walking down toward the sea together, clutching their mugs. In the kitchen, on the table, lay Matt's jacket with his keys, wallet and phone. She stopped dead and looked at the phone. Should she do this? She knew it was unwise, and she had to trust Matt if she was going to have a serious relationship with him, but she also needed a little reassurance; she needed to know that he was one of the good guys.

She picked up the phone. She knew the password was her name, so she keyed it in. Then she stopped and put the phone down; this was all wrong. She looked out the window at her mom and Matt; they had started walking down the beach to the rocks where she and Matt had sat and chatted for hours when she first got back. She had to know who he'd been texting. She scrolled through the texts. There were lots of messages to people at the club and various players, but more than anything, there were dozens of texts to Nancy. Nancy?

She opened the text he'd sent right after they had made love:

"Hi, can I come over on Monday... about 3:00 p.m.? It would be great if I could come through the back so Lisa doesn't see me. X"

Nancy replied immediately: "Yes, of course, darling, looking forward to seeing you. Don't worry, Lisa will never know about your little visits!"

Lisa could feel her heart pounding in her chest. Nancy? She put the phone down and looked out the window. Her mom and Matt were laughing together, sitting on the rocks. What an absolute shit. He had wormed into her family and her heart. All the time, he was having an affair with someone old enough to be his mom. Someone who, let's be honest, looked a lot like his mom. Lisa felt her eyes fill with tears as she thought about the two occasions she had seen him in the Manor House...how friendly and familiar he had seemed with Nancy. Fuck. Lisa was such an idiot. Nancy was a very attractive, very sophisticated and elegant woman. Why wouldn't he like her?

Lisa picked up the phone again and read the texts aloud. There could be no denying their meaning. She wasn't being paranoid; this was for real. Were all men like this? Would she ever meet someone who wasn't jumping into bed with someone else the minute her back was turned? Lisa closed the texts, shut the phone and put it back on his jacket. She glanced out the window. Matt was helping her mum up from the rocks; they were clearly coming back inside.

She ran through to the bedroom, took off her jeans and T-shirt, grabbed a towel and went into the bathroom—where she locked the door, put the plug back in and reran the bath, getting back into it as soon as she heard Matt and her mom talking in the kitchen.

"Lisa, Matt is here, you know?"

"Sorry, I'm still in the bath," she replied. "Can you tell him I'll call him later?"

Then she heard Matt calling through the door, "Lise, it's me. I just wondered whether you wanted to come to the game today. I can give you a lift there and was going to suggest you come and watch the game with me, sitting on the bench. I can tell you what's going on and introduce you to some of the laws of the game."

"No, Matt, it's OK. Thanks very much, but I've got a ton to do this afternoon. I'll see you at the party, OK?"

"Sure, OK. See you later. Enjoy your bath. Love you."

Lisa slid back into the water, letting it cover her face and wash away her tears.

ONCE MATT HAD LEFT, she clambered out of the bath and headed into her bedroom; she tried to stay calm. She knew her mom would be mad at her for not coming out to see Matt, and she knew she'd be grilled on her relationship with him. She didn't need any of it. She got dressed quickly and went out onto the beach through the patio doors of her bedroom, locking them behind her. She pushed her hands into the pockets of her fleece cardigan and walked up the beach, as far away from the house as she could get. She kept walking until she reached the cliffs and clambered over them, banging her knees and scratching her knuckles as she went.

Some young children were playing down on the sand below her, patting a giant beach ball between them, shaking with laughter and delight as they played. Life was so simple when you were young. Why did it have to get so damn hard?

Her work and her love life had both just collapsed beneath her.

Lisa was desperate for a glass of wine, in fact, any alcohol. She didn't need to drown her sorrows as much as take the edge off them for a while. Just a couple of glasses of wine, she'd head back home and talk it all through with her mom. Georgina had always been an imparter of wise words. She'd know exactly what to do. Lisa clambered over the rocks and walked briskly into the village, heading for the bar.

She arrived at Flip Flop bar a few minutes later and pushed down on the handle, leaning her body weight against the door to make it open. But as she was about to step into the bright, airy room, someone put their hand on the door to stop her. She spun around and looked straight at Peter.

"We must stop meeting like this," he said. "People will talk."

"Oh God, you're the second last person in the world I want to see right now," said Lisa.

The timing of their meeting was atrocious. Lisa was angry at Matt and keen to cast all thoughts of him from her mind. She wanted a glass of wine—nothing else.

"Well, I'm only your second most disliked person. That sounds like an improvement," he said.

She smiled, despite herself. He'd always had the ability to make her laugh.

"Can I buy you a coffee?" he asked. "Nothing else. Just a coffee. We have to live in the same village as one another. Let's have coffee like civilised human beings."

"You can't buy me a coffee," said Lisa, letting herself into the bar. But you can buy me a glass of wine."

Lisa took a sip of the wine and felt the sweet warmth of it run down her throat, into her stomach and radiate down through her limbs. It was as if her body was giving her a gentle reminder that she hadn't eaten all day. Be careful, Lisa; you'll get very drunk very quickly.

Unfortunately, Lisa wasn't listening to the warning.

CHAPTER 15

$\mathcal{M}$att looked up at the crowds crammed into the stadium. Music boomed out, cheerleaders danced, and a feeling of goodwill and excitement pervaded. Matt knew he should be delighted, but as he scanned the crowds looking for just one face, a sense of misery crept through him. Where was she? He caught sight of several people he knew, many waving at him as he gave them a thumbs up to indicate that the team was ready; he was ready, and this was going to be a great day. He saw Emma with Isabella and their parents. He glanced at either side of the small group. Lisa wasn't with them.

Matt understood that Lisa was busy at work, but there seemed to have been a shift in their relationship since that glorious day in the hotel. She'd seemed distant from then on. He thought that day would mark a change in their relationship for the better...that they would feel closer than ever and more bonded. But it seemed to have sunk altogether. How she'd behaved earlier had been so hurtful —not even to get out of the bath to say hello to him when he'd gone over there, especially to see her? Why would she do that?

· · ·

LISA SMILED AND NODDED. "YES, PLEASE," she said.

"Or we could get something to eat?" said Peter.

"No, I just want to drink. I want to forget all about Nancy and everyone."

"What on earth has Nancy done?" asked Peter.

"Shhhh…" said Lisa. "Mustn't mention Nancy. It's all a big secret. Make sure you come through the back door to avoid her." Lisa was drunk; she knew she was drunk and didn't give a damn.

Peter ruffled her hair. "Come on, let's go back to my place. I've got lots of wine, lots of nibbles; you can tell me what's wrong."

He was being so nice to her, like a kind friend who wanted the best for her. She stood up and put on her fleece jacket.

"I have to go somewhere first," she said, crashing into the table in front of them. Maisie, the manageress, came over to her. "Are you OK, love?" she asked. "Need a hand?"

"She's fine," said Peter.

"I wasn't asking you. Lisa, are you OK?"

"I'm fine. I need to go to the ladies."

Maisie walked over to the bathrooms with Lisa. "Let me walk you home. Honestly, you don't want to leave here with that snake."

"I know. I know," said Lisa. "But all men are fucking snakes. Why does it matter which one you're with? They all hiss gently, then swing round and bite you and poison you."

"They're not all snakes. There are nice men around. Lots of nice men."

"Yeah, right."

They arrived at the toilets, and Lisa staggered into the cubicle while Maisie waited outside. "I can get Will to drop you back in the car if you like. We're so quiet here at the moment. Shall I get him to do that?"

"No," said Lisa, emerging from the cubicle and smiling at Maisie. "You are so beautiful," she said. "You are like Audrey Hepburn with your short brown hair and big brown eyes. Except you look better than her because you're alive, and she's dead."

"Thank you," said Maisie, slightly unsure whether being favourably compared to a dead woman was praise or not. "Sit down here, and I'll go and get Will."

Lisa sat, but as soon as Maisie moved round to the other side of the bar in search of her husband, Peter walked over to Lisa, helped her to her feet, and escorted her out of the bar. "Let's go," he said as he swung the door open with one arm, holding tightly onto Lisa with the other.

On the street outside, it seemed cold after the bar's warmth and the drink's warming effects. She pulled her fleecy jacket around her. Peter draped an arm around her shoulders as they walked towards Top Street, past Isabelle's hairdressing salon and onto Peter's flat. Lisa had never been there before. It was a place he had acquired after their break up after she'd flown to Scotland.

"Lisa, you so know what I did to you was the biggest mistake of my life, don't you? You have no idea how much I regret my actions. I've hated myself every day since it happened. I love you. I know I hurt you, but I love you, and I'll never hurt you again. Never. Please can we try again?"

"I don't know," she said. She felt very drunk now but wanted one more glass of wine. After that, she would go home.

Peter opened the front door and stood back, allowing Lisa to enter.

He could hardly contain his delight at what was happening. This was something he had never imagined. He knew he could be persuasive. He was a lawyer, for God's sake; that's what he did for a living. He also knew that Lisa was quite vulnerable and trusting, but he never thought he'd have a second chance with her after what he'd done. He was determined never to let her down again.

"Try!" shouted Isabella as, all around her, the stadium shook with excitement. She was really getting into this rugby business. She loved the drama and excitement of it. They'd never been a particularly sporting family, and she had no real interest in the technical intricacies of the sport. Still, it couldn't be topped as a crowd pleaser and a beautiful afternoon out. That's why she was amazed that Lisa wasn't there. If Isabella had been dating Matt, she would be here all the time, supporting him and involving herself in his life. Matt was such a lovely guy; what was Lisa doing? She loved her sister dearly but struggled to understand her.

Isabella waved at Matt and gave him a thumbs up, and he waved back, clenching his fist in the air to show his delight.

LISA WASN'T THINKING about Matt or rugby. The only thing she was thinking was that she might be making a huge mistake by being here, in Peter's flat. Even in her drunken state, she realised that she was making a terrible mistake as she took in the formal, logical layout of the place, the lack of home comforts, and the order all around. There were no cushions, flowers, photographs, or ornaments...no joy. How on earth had she ended up in this house with the plain cream walls and the awful leather sofas that reminded her of car seats? I mean - it was lovely, to the extent that it looked as if it had been put together from the pages of a magazine, untouched by thought or kindness, like a sterile hotel room.

As soon as the idea of a hotel room entered her mind, she thought of Matt. Their lovely afternoon. The happiness she'd felt. Oh God, what was she doing?

She'd come here with Peter today because she felt desperate - lonely and in need of company; he was a familiar face. He was someone who she'd had a relationship with for years. He was safe. Now that she was here, though, it felt wrong. Perhaps she'd go to sleep now. She lay back on the sofa and closed her eyes.

'YEEEEESS!" shouted Isabella, throwing her arms into the air. "Winners, winners, winners, winners," she began chanting along with the crowd. The match had been brilliant; the team had been brilliant. 36-0. Amazing. Blimey, she was turning into a real fan. Who'd have thought? She looked down onto the pitch, where Matt was running around, congratulating all the players. She was dying to catch his eye and tell him how well he'd done, but he was too absorbed in the melee on the pitch. So Isabella went back to chanting instead. "Winners, Winners, Winners,' she screamed.

LISA OPENED HER EYES. She lay on the sofa, the leather sticking to her bare arms. Why were her arms bare? She was wearing just her t-shirt. This wasn't what she wanted. She could feel his breath on her cheek as he moved closer, running his hands through her hair and telling her how beautiful she had looked that night in the red dress and how much he regretted what he had done.

"Everyone can make one mistake," he was saying. "That was my mistake; I will never make a mistake like that again. We'll be together forever now. I'll never let you down."

Lisa fought to sit up, her head spinning and a dull pain developing behind her eyes. How much had she drunk? They'd had two bottles in the bar; had they had more drinks here? She couldn't remember. She felt awful. The room twisted a turned around her. The feeling of his hands in her hair and his breath on her cheek began to annoy and irritate her.

"I'm going to kiss you," he said. Lisa tried to wave him off, but the effort involved in steadying the room left little energy for warding off Peter's advances. She felt his hand move down her shoulders, take her hands and lift them above her head. Then his hands returned to her waist as if to remove her top; she summoned all her energy to push him away and scrabble to her feet.

"Home," she said. "I want to go home."

"But we're having a lovely time," said Peter softly. "Sit down for a minute."

Lisa went to sit down and missed the edge of the sofa, landing in a heap on the floor. Peter leaned into her as if he were going to help her to her feet, but instead, he shoved his mouth against hers and kissed her. She shouted at him to stop, but nothing seemed to work. The room was tangling and spinning.

She pushed hard against him and shouted. "No."

Peter stopped. He looked at her, and though the world spun around her and the banging in her head was reaching obscene proportions, she felt calm. The pestering had come to an end.

"What's wrong," he said gently. "I don't understand. There's nothing to worry about. I'll never cheat on you again. We're going to be together forever."

"I need to go home," she said, staggering to her feet and gathering her things together. Peter was standing by the door.

"I'll drive you," he said.

"You can't drive," she said, "You've drunk way too much."

"I hardly drank a thing," he replied. "Come on. I'll drive you."

Lisa was confused. How could she be so rip-roaringly drunk while he was sober enough to drive? She followed him to the car, feeling sheepish and a bit stupid but relieved to be going home.

CHAPTER 16

*I*sabella was washing the dishes in the kitchen when she heard the car pull up outside. Her parents had popped out for a drink after the game, and she was expecting them any minute with a large Chinese takeaway. But it wasn't her parents' car outside... it was another car. She recognised it from somewhere.

It took her a while to place the fancy vehicle. Then it struck her; it was Peter's car. Would he never learn? Had he not picked up on the fact that his relationship with Lisa was over? Lisa wasn't interested; she'd met someone else and had moved on. There was no room for Peter in her life now. Isabella watched as he turned the car around.

Then she saw the passenger door open and saw Lisa step out. What the hell was going on? Isabella left her station by the sink, dropping the pan she'd been scrubbing into the soapy water, letting it splash up all over her as she walked toward the front door. She arrived there as Lisa appeared on the other side.

"What the hell?" asked Isabella, unable to finish a sentence before Lisa barged past her into her bedroom and collapsed onto the bed. Isabella followed, her wet hands dripping all over the wooden floor as she went.

"Lisa, what are you doing?"

"I'm not doing anything," said Lisa.

"I just don't understand," said Isabella. "You've met a fantastic new guy who worships the ground you walk on, and you're off with the guy who dumped you and broke your heart. It doesn't make any sense to me at all."

"Perhaps you know nothing about being in love then," said Lisa. "I know you all think Matt is wonderful, gorgeous and perfect, but he's not. He is exactly like Peter. I might as well have the original than some poor imitation." Lisa's head was spinning as she spoke. She felt awful.

"What are you talking about?" asked Isabella, sitting on the edge of Lisa's bed.

"Matt is having an affair, the same way that Peter had an affair."

"No, he's not," said Isabella. "He's simply not."

"I've seen the texts he has been sending to Nancy. I've read about the love affair they're having. I've read in detail about their attempts to keep it from me. He is not the golden, wonderful boy everyone thinks he is."

"I don't believe that," said Isabella, a confused look covering her face. "I just don't get it at all. He's not having an affair with Nancy. How could he? She's twice his age. You must have misunderstood. He loves you; he wants to be with you more than anything."

"No, you're wrong. I've seen the texts. I'm not an idiot. Please, can you leave me on my own?"

Isabella shrugged, stood up and walked towards the door.

"Before I go, tell me one thing - did you sleep with Peter tonight?"

"No, of course, I didn't," said Lisa. "How could you think I would? I drank too much, and he tried to kiss me, and I pushed him off. That's all."

Isabella went to her room and got herself ready for the evening ahead. She would try and persuade Lisa to come to the party tonight to talk to Matt, and if she didn't come, then Isabella would talk to him and urge him to speak to Lisa about this alleged affair. This was all becoming so ridiculous now.

Once she was ready, she knocked on Lisa's door. "I'm going to the club to join the others for the post-game party. I think you should come with me."

"No," said Lisa; everything was still spinning, and she felt awful.

"It'll be fun. They won today. Why don't you just come for one drink?"

"No," said Lisa. "Thank you for being so kind, Izzy, but I don't feel well."

"Have an aspirin and a glass of water. You'll feel better then. And you can talk to Matt and try and clear the air. "

"No, I'm not going to come.'

'I'm sure Matt would love to see you.'

'If Matt wants company, he can always call Nancy," said Lisa, rolling over and wrapping herself in the duvet.

"OK, have it your way," said Isabella, and Lisa heard the clicking of her heels on the ground and the sound of the door slamming.

Silence.

But then, a few minutes later, Lisa heard a gentle noise. It wasn't Isabella - she was too noisy. She listened and was sure she could hear someone moving around but with such a light touch across the carpet that it was barely audible. Then there was a gentle knock on her bedroom door and Sophia's voice.

"Want a coffee?" her older sister asked.

"That would be lovely," said Lisa, knowing that's exactly what she needed. "Thank you." Her voice was still shaky, and Sophia could tell something was wrong.

"Are you OK?" she asked.

"No," said Lisa, then she burst into tears. Lisa's relationship with Sophia was funny. The two sisters were so different, but it had been Sophia to whom she had turned whenever anything had gone wrong over the years.

Sophia opened the bedroom door and saw her sister lying on the bed.

"What is the matter?" she asked.

Lisa looked at the ceiling and then turned around to face her sister, who looked particularly beautiful in her '50s-style black shift dress and matching cropped black jacket with fur around the collar and cuffs.

"You look like a movie star," said Lisa.

Sophia smiled and patted her sister's hand. "Tell me what's wrong."

"Matt is having an affair with Nancy," Lisa said bluntly. "And, before you tell me I'm nuts, I read it in his texts. I shouldn't have looked through his texts, but I knew something was up. He was texting and not telling me who he was texting, and I felt the whole Peter thing happening again. I had to find out what was happening, so I went onto his phone and saw it all."

"Have you been drinking?" asked Sophia.

"Yes, but that was after I saw the texts. I was completely sober when I saw them."

"And you couldn't have misunderstood what the text was all about?"

"Oh, God," said Lisa. "You sound exactly like Isabella. Of course, I understand what they meant. He's having an affair, and I'm a fucking idiot."

"What did they say?" asked Sophia, sitting on the edge of Lisa's bed.

"They talked about the two meeting up and how they had to keep it a secret from me. And it's not just the tests; Matt's been there twice to see her. I saw him go in, and he wouldn't tell me why he was there."

"I didn't know Matt knew Nancy."

'Neither did I until I bumped into him in her kitchen."

"I'm sorry, sweetheart. But you know you need to talk to Matt about all this, don't you? There may be a straightforward explanation."

"Yeah, right," said Lisa, bursting into tears. "I think we all know what the explanation is."

Sophia stroked Lisa's hair. "Is there anything I can do?" she asked.

"Actually, there is something, but you're not going to like this…."

"OK, try me," said Sophia.

"I'd like you to take me to the airport."

"You're joking," said Sophia. "No, you can't run away again. For God's sake, call Matt and ask him to come here and talk to you. Tell him what you've seen. If he doesn't respond or responds badly, then, by all means, get on the next plane. But surely you owe it to him and all of us to talk to him first."

"Sophia, you asked me whether there was anything you could do for me, and I've told you. If you won't take me, that's fine. I'm just in a mess. I saw Peter tonight, and it fucked me up. And I don't want to see Matt, and I don't want to talk to Matt. And I hate Peter. He knew how drunk I was and had his hands all over me. And I feel like shit, and I have to get out of here."

CHAPTER 17

*I*sabella pushed her way through the crowds at the bar, trying to get to Matt. The incredible victory had made him the most popular man in the county. Well-wishers surrounded him, so no one else could get near. For the first time, Isabella noticed how many cheerleaders gathered around him—there was a puff of sparkles and sequins following him wherever he went. All of them the colour of freshly polished beech wood, with their white skirts, dizzy blonde hair and enormous, lipstick-enhanced smiles.

"Have you got a minute?" Isabella shouted over to him. It wasn't the time or the place, but she couldn't let this go.

"Of course," he said. "What's up? Is Lisa here?"

"No, Matt, I think there's a problem. Can we go outside?"

Matt led Isabella through the crowds of fans and out to the car park, where they'd have some peace and quiet.

"She came home tonight upset and said you were having an affair."

Matt's face immediately told her that Lisa had got this all wrong. He looked incredulous.

"Why on earth would she think I was having an affair?"

"I don't know. But she's convinced that you and Nancy are sleeping together."

"Nancy? What on earth are you talking about?"

"I don't really know, Matt, but something about texts you sent to Nancy about coming to see her and not wanting Lisa to find out? I think she must have looked through your phone."

"Oh, for God's sake," said Matt, dropping his head into his hands. "She's got this all wrong. Why would she need to look through my texts in the first place?"

"She's been badly hurt," said Isabella. "I guess she was nervous and keen to ensure you weren't lying to her."

"Fucking hell."

It was odd to hear Matt swear. He wasn't someone who swore a lot.

"Is she coming here tonight?" he asked Isabella.

"She's lying on her bed crying, Matt. She's not going anywhere."

"OK. I'll go and see her. Let me get a cab."

"I can drive you," said Isabella, fishing in her handbag for her keys.

"Thank you," he said, dialling Lisa's number.

LISA REJECTED the call and sat back in the passenger seat of Sophia's car. She didn't want to talk to Matt now—not ever if the truth be known. They were finished. It was all over. She wanted nothing to do with him. She had called Charlie and told her that she needed to escape once again—and Charlie had laughed at first, then heard the pain in her voice and told her to get on the next plane to Scotland. The last plane was at 11, and she would make it by a whisker.

"We will get there on time, won't we?" she asked Sophia.

"Yes, don't worry. But are you sure you don't want to talk to Matt first? At least explain why you're so upset...why you're running away. He's a reasonable guy, Lise. This isn't like it was with Peter. You can talk to Matt."

"No thanks," she said. Her phone was on silent, but she could feel it constantly vibrate as Matt tried to call her. "I don't want to call him. I want nothing to do with him."

· · ·

By the time Sophia returned from dropping Lisa at the airport, the last thing she wanted to do was go to the party, so she headed straight for home, entering the house quietly and preparing to creep into her bedroom so as not to wake her parents, who were surely at home and asleep by now. She'd update them in the morning. At least Lisa had promised that she was only going for a couple of days this time, and she had sworn that she would call both Nancy and Matt to talk about what she had seen.

But far from needing to creep into a quiet house, Sophia was astonished to hear voices in the living room—the sound of male and female voices. It wasn't just her mom and dad. Sophia walked in to see Isabella and Matt talking to her parents. As she walked in, Matt jumped up.

"Have you seen Lisa?" he asked.

Oh, God. She had been hoping to delay this until the morning.

"She's on her way to Edinburgh," said Sophia sheepishly. She was worried they'd blame her or at least feel that she should have spoken to them before whisking her off. "I had to take her…I had no choice," added Sophia. "She begged me not to call anyone. She's only gone for a couple of days."

"I'm going after her," said Matt, stepping past Sophia and heading for the door.

"It was the last flight," said Sophia. "You won't be able to go now."

Peter strutted around his apartment. What the fuck had that been about?

She knew how much he cared about her; she'd come to his apartment quite willingly—and, yes, he'd kept filling up her wine glass and pushing her to drink while he himself was completely sober, but he had done her no harm. He had behaved in an entirely gentlemanly fashion. So why had she suddenly wanted to go home? It had seemed to him that the evening was heading only one way…back to a relationship.

Why had she run away like that?

Perhaps he should have stopped her going?

Surely, she could see that they were destined to be together. He sat in the leather armchair and saw her pink scarf tucked down the side of the cushions. He pulled it out and smelled it. Pine trees. It was such a familiar smell that he was transported back to the days when they lived together, and everything was wonderful. Perhaps if he were to turn up now with the scarf, all would be well again.

Perhaps they would slip back into a relationship, and it would be like his little dalliance with the dancer never happened. It would be fine. She had never found out about his previous dalliances, and he would be cautious and make sure she found out about none of the future ones. He wanted her back - she was a good influence on him, a good supporter, and he missed her being there.

Peter left his apartment and headed for his car, clutching the pink scarf between his fingers, smelling it every so often and letting the scent take him back to a happier, simpler time when his future was planned, organised and settled. He knew what he must do. He turned the key in the ignition and pointed his car towards that lovely but scruffy, lemon-coloured house on the beach.

MATT COULDN'T WORK out whether to be mad at himself or Lisa. He was cross that she seemed to have so little trust in him that she would go into his phone and read his texts. Equally, he was cross with himself for creating a situation that could be so severely misinterpreted.

The truth was that he was planning to buy Suffolk Manor from Nancy, and he didn't want to let Lisa know until the whole thing was signed off. Now it had backfired spectacularly. He looked through the texts; it was easy to see why she had misconstrued them. They read as if he were having an affair with Nancy, and he could see quite how that would throw Lisa into a tailspin. She had been so hurt before; she would mistrust easily.

The texts, which appeared to be organising some sort of assignation with Nancy, were never written for Lisa to see. They were written because he was trying to protect her and to make the relationship as real as possible before he revealed that he was buying Suffolk Manor. He hadn't wanted to tell Lisa immediately because it was pretty complicated; he would end up being her boss. He needed to handle it carefully.

"I'll drive to Scotland. I'll be there by morning."

"You can't drive, Matt; you've been drinking," said Sophia.

"I'll get a driver then. I hate flying anyway. I'll be in Edinburgh first thing. Tell me where Charlie's apartment is, and I'll be outside as soon as they wake up."

"Listen, Matt, why don't you get an early flight? I'll pick you up in the morning and drop you at the airport. You can fly to Edinburgh, and you'll be there by midmorning," said Isabella.

"I want to be there before mid-morning," said Matt. "I want to be there to see her as soon as she opens her eyes. I want to be able to reassure her and tell her that everything's all right. I'm one of the good guys, you know."

"Yes, we know that," said Sophia. "We all know that very well."

The sound of a car pulling up outside temporarily distracted them from the task of dissuading Matt from booking a driver. He sat back down on the sofa with a huge sigh. Then he sat bolt upright. What if Lisa had changed her mind or missed the last flight?

He rushed towards the front door with Isabella in hot pursuit. Matt swung the door open, and there stood Peter. It took Matt a moment to realise who it was, and then it dawned on him. The shiny shoes, the glossy hair, the fancy clothes. It was Peter. Who has time to polish their shoes until they shine like that?

"I'm Peter," said the shiny-shoe man.

"I'm Matt."

"Oh. Nice to meet you," said Peter, extending an arm clad in some expensive mohair, cashmere, or something. His hands were small for a man's, and his fingernails were perfect ovals. Matt shook the hand, deriving significant pleasure from squeezing harder than one normally would. He saw Peter wince and congratulated himself. He could crush this man in seconds.

"I was just returning this," said Peter. "Lisa left it in my apartment earlier."

"She was in your apartment earlier?" asked Matt, his voice both louder and deeper than it should have been. "What the hell was she doing in your apartment?"

"We went out for a drink, and she came back for more drinks at my place afterwards. I'm her former fiancé; don't look so shocked."

But Matt was shocked.

"What the hell was Lisa doing with this clown with the shiny shoes?" asked Matt, turning to Isabella.

"They're Gucci," muttered Peter defensively.

"They were just talking," said Isabella. "Nothing to worry about."

"You knew about this?"

"Well, yes. Peter brought her home earlier."

"I don't believe this. I don't understand any of it. I'm in trouble for trying to buy a beautiful house and not wanting Lisa to know until it's all sorted out. She's spending the evenings with this idiot, and everyone seems to think that's OK."

Matt stepped forward to grab Peter by the throat, but Lisa's dad stepped in.

"Not in my house," he said calmly but with absolute authority. "You will not fight in front of my wife and daughters. Have more dignity...both of you."

The two men, silenced by Donald's words, continued to glare at one another.

"Where's Lisa?" asked Peter.

"She's in Edinburgh. She's gone back to stay with Charlie again," said Isabella.

"I'm going to Edinburgh," said Peter.

"No, I'm going to Edinburgh," said Matt.

"Oh, just stop it!" yelled the girls' mom, in an almighty voice that belied her tiny frame. "Both of you, stop it now. My daughter is upset and missing, and all you two care about is your egos."

"But I love her," said Peter, in a manner made all the more pathetic by the whiny voice that accompanied it.

"If you loved her, you wouldn't have gone off with the first woman who turned your head. She's not interested in you and never will be."

Peter's shoulders dropped; it was as if they'd been full of air and someone had stuck a pin in them.

"You should go," said Sophia. "Go. Find someone new. Move on."

Peter gave a weak half-smile to Sophia and turned slowly, sauntering drearily toward his car with all the determination and joy of someone walking toward a firing squad. Then he got to his vehicle, wound down the window and smiled at the assembled group. "Did you think I'd give up this easily?" he asked. "I mean – really? If anyone wants me, I'll be in Edinburgh."

MATT MOVED to chase after Peter's departing car as Donald reached out and grabbed him. "Stop this," he said. Their father didn't involve himself much in the detail of their lives, but this was his house, and they would behave with respect. "Can someone please tell me what is going on?"

"Lisa thinks Matt is having an affair with Nancy," said Isabella.

"But I'm not," chipped in Matt.

"Why does she think you're having an affair with this woman?"

"Because I sent Nancy texts, and Lisa misinterpreted them. I'm not having an affair with anyone, Mr Lopez. I love your daughter."

A silence descended on the room.

"I think you should get on the first plane to Edinburgh in the morning," said Donald. "Let's have no more talk about driving to Edinburgh at midnight."

"But…"

"No," said Lisa's father firmly. "I know my daughter; she needs a little time to herself. Go tomorrow."

"I can't - what if Peter goes to Edinburgh? I need to go."

"Don't worry about him," said Isabella. "He'll go to the airport tonight, realise there are no more flights to Edinburgh, and that will be the end of it. Trust me, Matt, he's not worth worrying about."

.   .   .

PETER GRIPPED the steering wheel hard as he drove away from the cottage. He felt angry and very frustrated. She'd caught him out in one little mistake. All he'd been doing was having sex with a woman. Big wow! Did she really think he was the first man ever to be unfaithful? Then she flew off to Edinburgh, and no one would tell him where she'd gone. It was ridiculous.

He'd been so pleased when he heard that Lisa was returning to Cove Bay, and he'd been quietly confident that he could convince her to return to him. But then this bloody guy Matt had turned up. Who was he? Some jumped up jock without a penny or a brain cell to his name.

Peter called the airport as he drove away from Lisa's house. "No more flights tonight."

Bollocks.

He didn't want to drive to Edinburgh, it would take all night, but he couldn't let that meathead get there first. He rang Ross, the young assistant they had just taken on at the law firm. The guy was enthusiastic and ambitious. He'd do whatever Peter asked him to.

"Want to do something that will help your career?" he asked.

"Yes, sir," said Ross. Peter could hear the delight in his voice.

"I need you to drive me to Edinburgh tonight."

"Tonight?" said Ross, the enthusiasm draining out of his voice.

"Is that a problem?" said Peter. "Perhaps I should talk to one of the other trainees?"

"Not at all," said Ross. "I'm ready to go when you are."

CHAPTER 18

"Welcome back! You just couldn't keep away, could you?" said Charlie, wrapping her arms around Lisa and kissing her on the cheek. "What the hell has happened now?"

"It's a disaster," said Lisa, looking at her friend and bursting into tears. "It's all a complete and utter disaster, and I don't know why or how."

"Come on, let's get you home, and you can tell me all about it."

THE STREET LIGHTS flickered through raindrops as Lisa sat in the passenger seat of Charlie's car. The music bounced along as they meandered through the traffic, windscreen wipers whirring and Charlie beside her, offering comfort and words of support. Despite the noise, warmth and company of Charlie, Lisa felt terrible. Her insides tugged in on themselves; an ache of loneliness silently gripped her as the city danced and partied around them.

It had been bad the last time she'd come to Edinburgh, with thoughts of Peter and his betrayal pounding in her head, but this time it felt so much worse. Last time she'd felt betrayed, angry and embarrassed; she'd been concerned that her future life had been snatched away. This time it felt like her heart would break into two.

"I know you must think I'm bonkers coming back here, saying I'm in love with someone else and that he's having an affair too, but it's true."

"A little bit bonkers," said Charlie affectionately. "But mainly, I understand. You're such a romantic little thing."

"This guy's the real deal," she said. "He's lovely. Or, I thought he was until I discovered he'd been sleeping with Nancy. Do you remember her? Remember how old she is? He must be just after her for money. His parents are rich, and he's not. Perhaps he thinks he'll marry someone rich to impress his cold, soulless mother. Do you know the bizarre thing? Nancy looks a bit like his mother...how bloody freaky is that?"

"Pretty freaky, angel," said Charlie. "But don't worry; we'll be home soon. I propose hot chocolate and Baileys with red velvet cake. Nothing feels so bad when your face is covered in red velvet cake and your throat is coated in chocolate and Baileys.

MAX STAGGERED in from his night out to see Lisa sitting on the sofa, crying into an empty glass of Bailey's while Charlie hunted for the bottle in the kitchen. Max looked at her, exactly as he had done months previously when he'd first met her: a sad and heartbroken woman struggling to make sense of what had happened.

"Hello again," he slurred with a boyish grin. "You're back!"

"I am," said Lisa, wiping her eyes and repeating the story for his benefit. Max listened patiently, running a hand through her hair to calm her when she became upset.

"Are you sure you haven't misunderstood these texts?" he said. "I mean, tell me to shut up if I'm wrong, but he hasn't actually *done* anything wrong. It's not like Peter. He was a dick - forever delaying the wedding and shagging someone on his desk. I mean - he had trouble written all over him. This guy, though? I'm not so sure. Texts can be hard to decipher. Could you have got it all wrong, Lisa?"

"No, Max, I haven't got it wrong. He's a rugby coach used to women throwing themselves at him. I bet they threw themselves at him when he was a player, and they still do now. You should see those cheerleaders...they are so beautiful it's ridiculous. Matt's used to having women fall at his feet. Screwing some old bird's no big deal to him."

"What's his name? I know all about rugby; perhaps I've heard of him," said Max.

"Matt Rowls," said Lisa. "He retired a few years ago and has been coaching the local side."

"You're joking!" said Max. "*The* Matt Rowls?"

"I don't know," said Lisa. "His name's Matt Rowls. Why? Have you seen him play? He was quite good in his time."

"Good?" said Max. "Good? He was amazing. Brilliant for Scotland. I was such a big fan. You must have heard of him?"

Lisa looked at him blankly.

"Well, you will have to take it from me...your boyfriend was a rugby sensation. He retired too early because he had chronic injuries, but that guy...hell, Lisa. He was a superhero. And he bought a load of property in Scotland, I think. And he let these homeless people stay in one of the houses. I'm sure that was Matt. I'll google it later, but - yeah. Matt Rowls. Blimey. What the hell is he doing in Cove Bay?"

"The team from Exeter has moved to Salcombe. He's the manager of the club."

Max was scrolling through his phone. "Oh yes - here it is 'Rowls set to take rugby to Devon seaside resort.' Wow. Bloody hell."

"Well done him. If he were a superhero, you'd think he wouldn't have to screw fifty-year-old women. I'm going to bed."

CHAPTER 19

*L*isa woke early and looked through the window and down at
the traffic crawling past outside. It all seemed so dark and
harsh. Car horns, people shouting, the insistent beeping of a
lorry reversing and police cars wailing as they fought to get through
the morning traffic.

It was so unlike home, where she looked out at the beach and the
sea. The views at Cove Bay were light, life-giving, warm and happy.
The place seemed to offer softness and serenity. Here people were
almost zombie-like as they pounded the streets. She didn't remember
it being like this before. She watched them and thought about how
wonderful her life back home was...her kind family and her fantastic
job. It was so frustrating that it had disappeared now. How could she
possibly go there and work for Nancy when the woman was sleeping
with her boyfriend?

"WANT BREAKFAST?" asked Charlie, peering into the room. "There is a
fancy new French cafe just across the street."

"New cafe?" asked Lisa. "Shit...I've only been away for a few weeks;
how the hell has a new place opened up?"

"You know what Edinburgh is like... There are always changes going on, new things coming, old things going. The arrival of the new and constant reinvention is one of the best things about living here. It's vibrant and fresh. Now get up lazy-bones, and let's go eat."

Things changed so quickly in this big city: new places and new people created a vibrancy. That's what was special about city life. Things never stayed the same... they changed and swung and blossomed. Things grew bigger and better all the time.

The French-style cafe was packed with Edinburgh's finest, ordering coffee to go or sitting down to a variety of continental breakfasts. Lisa and Charlie ignored the French theme and ordered big Scottish breakfasts and bottomless cups of coffee. They found a spot at a corner table and sat down.

It was so noisy they could hardly hear one another speak. The clatter of plates and the sound of people coming in through the door were so loud they had to shout to raise their voices above the din.

"Wasn't that weird last night?" said Charlie. "Max knowing exactly who Matt was and saying how good he was. It really made me laugh how much of a fan Max was."

Lisa laughed. "Yes, that was funny. I don't think he thought I was telling the truth when I first said Matt's name. I had no idea that Matt was such a big star. Oh, I know what it says on Google, and I've seen him on Wikipedia, but they are just words, and hearing that he won this tournament and was in that team doesn't mean all that much when you're not a rugby fan. It was very funny to see Max's little face light up, and when he said he wanted an autograph, I thought I was going to die laughing."

"You seem much happier today," said Charlie. "I'm really glad."

"Yes…must be something about Edinburgh. I don't like cities at all. I don't even like going to Plymouth. It's all so noisy, brash, fast and impersonal, but it is a complete escape. Coming here has allowed me to think clearly in a way that I never would have if I'd stayed there."

"I get that. But your family must be worried about you - dropping everything and flying up here again."

"Sophia's face was a picture," said Lisa. "She just couldn't believe it when I asked her to take me to Exeter airport."

"Have you called Matt? Have you explained what you saw and why you ran away?"

Lisa hadn't. She hadn't turned her phone on since she'd been in Edinburgh. She couldn't bear the thought of hearing him confirm her worst thoughts. She explained this to Charlie and watched her friend's eyebrows raise.

"You have to put your phone on. He's probably been ringing non-stop."

"I don't want to," Lisa said. "I really can't face talking to him."

"OK, I understand that, but you don't have to talk to him…just put your phone on at least and see whether he's called."

Lisa turned her phone on and watched as it burst to life with four-teen missed calls—ten of them from Matt, two from her home number and two from Peter. She groaned when she saw Peter's name on the screen. He wasn't important…she needed to ignore him and to call her mom, calm her down and tell her she was OK.

Then the texts appeared, coming through one by one - all from Matt. He was begging her to call him, telling her he could explain everything. What sort of creative story would he invent to cover that one up?

The phone bleeped again - a text from Sophia, urging her to call. Her breakfast arrived, and Lisa put the phone down on the table, turning to Charlie. "I'll call him after this, promise," she said.

They ate their breakfast in silence, devouring the bacon and eggs, and ordering more coffees.

"Perhaps I should text Matt? That would be easier."

"Yes, but it's not about being easier; it's about being fair," said Charlie. "He deserves the chance to explain."

As they sipped their coffee, Lisa's phone bleeped again, and again, and again.

She picked it up.

"My money's on Matt," said Charlie, shaking her head.

"Oh no," said Lisa, feeling the blood drain from her face.

"What's the matter?"

"A whole load of texts from Peter have just come through."

"Peter? What - old fiancé Peter?"

"Yes," said Lisa nervously.

"What does he want? You haven't seen him for months."

"Oh, God. There's something I haven't told you," she said, shifting nervously in her seat.

"What on earth have you done? Don't tell me you slept with Peter."

"No."

"What?" asked Charlie.

"I didn't sleep with him, but I was with Peter last night."

"What? Are you serious?"

"Yes… I was a mess. I saw the texts on Matt's phone, and I freaked out and ran off. I bumped into Peter. I didn't do anything wrong, but I know it's going to look bad."

"Christ, Lisa, you don't make it easy for yourself, do you?"

Lisa shook her head as her phone bleeped again.

She picked it up and burst into tears.

"Peter's in Edinburgh," she said. "He drove here during the night. He wants to see me."

Charlie dropped her head into her hands. "We'll see the funny side of this one day," she said.

Lisa wasn't so sure. If Matt found out that Peter had come to Edinburgh, he'd think that Lisa had invited him. God, this was awful.

"I think I've messed things up with Matt," she said. "If he hears Peter is here, he'll…"

"Right. Be honest with me: do you want to get back with Peter?" asked Charlie.

"No! Definitely not," said Lisa. "Christ, no. Why would you even think that?"

"Because you used to be engaged to him, were heartbroken when he called it off, and now you admit to having spent yesterday evening with him."

"I don't want him. I want Matt."

"Then call Matt."

"But what about the fact that Peter is...."

"CALL MATT."

Lisa dialled Matt's number, but it went straight to voicemail.

"I'll call him again as soon as we get back to the flat," said Lisa. As she spoke, her phone rang, and Sophia's number appeared on the screen. She couldn't face talking to her yet. "I'll call her when we get back to the apartment as well," she said, cutting off her sister.

Charlie looked at her. "Why did you run away instead of speaking to Matt?" she asked. "You say you like him, but now you don't seem to want to sort it out. I don't understand."

"I'm scared," said Lisa. "I'm scared that Matt is just as bad as Peter. Or, you know, that all men are actually just as bad as one another. I'm also worried that I've completely messed things up with Matt."

There was a pause while Lisa collected herself.

"I ran away because I was drunk and ashamed and because I'm rubbish at confrontations," she said to Charlie. She didn't know where the words had come from or even whether they were true, but she had said them.

Charlie smiled at her. "You did nothing wrong," she said.

"I went to my ex-fiancé's house and got very drunk. It's not model-girlfriend behaviour, really, is it?"

"No, but it's not model-boyfriend behaviour to have secret texts to someone. Hey, neither of you is perfect. Nobody's perfect. What a surprise."

Lisa smiled

"And as far as him being as bad as Peter - you didn't catch him having sex. There might be a totally rational explanation for the texts," said Charlie.

"There can't be," said Lisa. "I saw them."

"Tell me again what they said," said Charlie, then spotting the number of people around them, listening in, she changed her mind. "Come on - let's go for a walk. We can chat while we're strolling."

They walked down towards the cluster of fashion shops that Charlie loved and had failed to get Lisa interested in. "You should see the boots they've got in *Slice* - just fabulous - covered in graffiti," she said. "Shall we go and see them? I am so tempted to buy them."

While Charlie talked, Lisa looked around, completely distracted by the thought of Peter being in town and the fear that she might bump into him.

"We'll meet Max for an early supper later," said Charlie as the women walked down Prince's Street. Charlie's eyes were trained on the new dresses that had arrived. She commented on the soft leather jackets that had appeared in her favourite shops.

"These windows change every day," she said, full of excitement. "Honestly, I could spend every penny I earned in here. There "they are…those are the boots."

Lisa wasn't interested in clothes at the best of times, and this was, quite considerably, not the best of times.

"Let's go in," said Charlie, forging ahead into the shop and picking up the boots with such tenderness that it was like she was picking up a newborn baby. Then she began scanning the racks, looking for some white capri pants inspired—it seemed—by the ones that Lisa had brought with her. It must be the first time in Lisa's entire existence that she had inspired someone with her fashion choices.

Lisa moved loyally beside her friend, pretending to be interested in the racks of clothes but thinking only of Cove Bay and how she wished she was sitting on the beach now, looking out to sea, with Matt by her side. She thought back to the night they had sat there together after the barbecue with her family.

As she thought of the soft, damp sand, she felt her toes digging into the bottoms of her shoes as if she were curling them into the beach at home. She wrapped her arms around herself; she wanted to be home. She wanted to be with Matt. As she thought, her phone beeped. She pulled it out of her handbag to see a text from Matt. It was just one line.

"See you by Arthur's Seat in an hour."

"Charlie, look," cried Lisa. "Look at this."

"What have you found?" asked Charlie, relieved that her friend was at least looking at clothes and engaging a little in the day's activities.

But, when she turned around, Lisa was nowhere near the clothes; she was hurtling toward Charlie with her arms outstretched, clutching her mobile phone.

"Look," she repeated. "Look—a text."

You'd think the woman had never received a text before. "Who's it from?" asked Charlie.

"It's from Matt. I have to go. I'm seeing him in an hour. How do I get there?"

"You can walk there in 10/15 minutes, but why don't we go home, and you can get ready properly."

"No, I want to go now; point me in the right direction," said Lisa.

Charlie began to explain, and then Lisa was gone, running across the shop, heading for the door.

"Right, well, that seems to be sorted," said Charlie, talking to the boots. "Let's go and try you little lovelies on, shall we?"

"I really love him," Lisa shouted to Charlie as she ran blindly through the rails of clothing, almost taking out two teenage shoppers as she went. "I'll call you later."

Lisa arrived at the castle half an hour early and saw the queues of people waiting to go in. The last thing she wanted to do was stand in line for an hour and miss Matt. She dug into her purse and found the access pass that had allowed her to come in and tend to the gardens. It was a few months since she'd used it, but it was worth a try. She walked to the front of the queue and flashed it at the ticket office.

"In you go," said the guard.

Great, now she had to find Matt. Where would he be? Edinburgh Castle was a big place. She looked up at the sign

When she arrived, Matt was already standing at the top of the stairs, with magnificent views of Edinburgh stretching out behind him. He looked worried and nervous as she approached but strong and determined.

"Hi," she said. She had butterflies in her stomach and a smile on her face. It was an odd combination.

"What's going on?" he asked. "I just don't understand... You know how I feel about you; what are you doing?"

"I saw the texts," said Lisa. "I know I shouldn't have looked, but I was worried. Can we go and sit down?"

"Of course," said Matt, leading her back down and into the castle grounds. He removed his jacket and laid it on the ground so she could sit comfortably next to him.

"Thank you," she said. "But don't worry. I can sit on the grass; I don't want to get your jacket dirty."

"It's fine," said Matt. "Talk to me."

"When Peter was having an affair, he conducted the whole thing by text," said Lisa. "He would be on his phone, texting but refusing to tell me who he was contacting. I assumed it was people from work but had a real shock when I realised that all the time, he'd been conducting this affair.

"Obviously, I was devastated when I found out he was cheating on me, but I also felt stupid for trusting him and allowing him to treat me like that when I could see him texting all the time. I know this is unfair, and you're not Peter, but when you were texting in the hotel room and wouldn't tell me who you were texting, it brought it all back," Lisa tried to explain.

"So, you read the texts then?"

"No, the day you came over, and I was in the bath."

"What you read was me contacting Nancy," said Matt.

"Yes, and arranging to meet up with her and warning her that you would come through a private entrance so that I wouldn't see you."

"Because I didn't want you to know something... Oh, God... Lisa, this is so difficult... I'm buying Nancy's house. I'm the mystery buyer. The reason I'm in that tiny little one-bedroom apartment at the moment is that I'm planning to move into the big house.

"I didn't want to mention it to you because you'd be worried about how it would affect your job, how it would affect us and what would happen. I wanted to go ahead with the whole purchase and only tell you when I was sure it was mine. I had to beg my parents not to say anything, and I've asked Nancy not to say anything because it's not fair for you to discover that I'm your new boss so soon into a relationship.

I thought, in a few months, when we were more stable, it would be a better time to tell you when I knew I'd definitely got the house. Also - I didn't want you to think I was some flash idiot like Peter - waving his money around. I wanted you to fall in love with me and want to be with me for me, not because I'm a famous rugby player and not because I have a lot of money."

Lisa felt herself go weak. "Sorry. But you can rest assured that I had no idea you had any money at all - I thought you were quite poor, and I didn't know you were a famous rugby player until last night."

"Last night?"

"Oh, Charlie's brother Max knew who you were."

"OK, well, I'm only well-known in Scotland, to be honest. I made some money from rugby and invested it in property. That's how I can afford the house."

"It's the most beautiful house ever."

"I know, but it's not definite yet," said Matt. "The first time we met, on the plane, I'd been in Edinburgh sorting out all the finances. I was flying back to finish off the purchase, but there have been lots of little issues, as there often are with old houses. I've been trying to iron them out. I never envisioned you popping up and me falling hopelessly in love with you. I just thought it was better for you if I didn't say anything right away. I didn't know you were going to go to my phone and read my texts. That's a real betrayal of trust."

"I'm sorry."

"You have to trust me, or we have no relationship. I'm not going to cheat on you; I love you. And—by the way—did you really think I'd be having an affair with someone who was old enough to be my mother?"

"Well, I did think it was a bit odd..." said Lisa. "But she's always so elegant and smart, and the house is so beautiful. I thought maybe you'd overlooked the age. To be honest, I thought you had no money, and she had loads. I thought that might appeal to you or something...I don't know."

"Listen, Lisa; I need you to trust me. I need you to believe that I am a good person and am not going to hurt you or run off with anyone.

But I also need you to stop running away when you think things are going wrong. Don't fall back into Peter's arms; don't jump on a plane."

"I'd never fall into Peter's arms. Never. Not in a million years," said Lisa. "And I promise not to run away again. I do trust you. And I love you. I love you very much."

"Good," said Matt. "Now, let's put all this behind us, shall we? Put Peter behind us, and start focusing on the future."

"Okay," said Lisa. "But there's just one other thing…"

"Oh no. What?" asked Matt.

"Peter is in Edinburgh."

"He is here? What? With you?"

"No, not with me. He followed me out here."

"Bloody hell," said Matt. "I saw him at your house, looking for you, but I never thought he'd come. Have you seen him?"

"He was at my house?"

"Yes, last night. Your dad threw him out, and Peter said he was going to Edinburgh, but I didn't think for one minute that he meant it. I didn't realise he'd actually come here."

"Well, he did. He's here. He texted to tell me he'd arrived, and he has been ringing ever since, but I haven't taken his calls. I texted back to say that I wasn't interested. I said I was in love with you."

"Good," said Matt. "If he rings again, I'll talk to him."

"Thank you," said Lisa. "Now, come on - I think it's time I took you to meet Charlie."

CHAPTER 20

"*H*ere we are," said Charlie, pushing open the door to the head-splittingly trendy Edinburgh restaurant. Everyone in there was wearing black: the bar staff, the bouncers, all the men and all the women. Max was wearing black, and Charlie was wearing black. But not Lisa. Oh no. Lisa was wearing a bright yellow t-shirt with 'I wish I were in Cove Bay' printed on it, very untrendy baggy jeans and red Converse trainers.

"Will they let me in?" she said. "Look at everyone here... I've never seen so many terrifyingly cool people all together in one place."

"Of course, they'll let you in. You look post-cool and funky," said Charlie.

"Is that a thing?"

"Nope. I made it up, just take a seat and let's get some wine."

"Everyone's staring," said Lisa. "Look at that guy. I wish I'd worn black."

Charlie looked up and conceded that - yes - people did seem to be staring at them. Then finally, someone came over.

Oh God thought Lisa, they are going to chuck me out for not looking like a trendy, young architect.

"I'm sorry to interrupt your night," said the man. "Can I have a picture with you? I'm a huge fan."

"Sure," said Matt, posing next to the guy.

"I'll never forget that Six Nations match in 2015. My God, you were good."

"Ha, thanks. Yes - the England team crumbled a bit, didn't they?"

"No - they didn't crumble,m you guys were brilliant. Lovely to meet you. Thanks for the selfie."

The approach of the first guy signalled an avalanche of fans, all wanting to talk to Matt about that time when he led Scotland to victory or that time when he scored the greatest try ever."

"Blimey, you're properly famous," said Charlie. "It's not just Max who's a fan."

They were being approached from all sides by people wanting selfies and eager to remind him of 'that time' when they'd watched him perform magic with a rugby ball.

"We're never going to be able to eat our meals in peace, and where's the wine waiter?" said Charlie; the allure of being with someone famous had quickly faded when she realised she wouldn't be able to get a drink.

Max signalled to the maître d' that they needed help, and two waiters arrived to guide them to a secluded spot at the top end of the restaurant, looking down on the other diners without being disturbed by them.

"A bottle of champagne, courtesy of the management," said a waiter, arriving behind them.

"So, I guess you're famous in Edinburgh?" said Lisa.

Matt smiled. "I tend to be able to go around the place without too much hassle most of the time, but there seem to be a lot of rugby fans in tonight, and I played most of my best sport here. People get very passionate about it."

Lisa smiled to herself. She loved the fact that he'd never been at all showy with her, and she'd never had any idea how famous, or indeed, how wealthy he was. She was pleased that she had fallen in love with him when she thought he was a jobbing coach, living in a shabby one-bedroomed apartment.

"Can I order for us all?" said Charlie. "I've been here before and know which dishes to choose."

"Of course," said Matt. "Go ahead."

While Charlie called the waiter over and listed dish after dish of Korean food, Lisa felt her phone vibrating in her handbag. She had called her mum and sisters and told them that Matt was with her and everything was fine, so had no idea who it would be. Nancy perhaps? She opened her phone and looked at the screen.

Peter's name stared back at her.

Matt looked over and saw who was ringing.

"I think I should call him," he said, taking the phone off her and preparing to stand up. "I need to speak to this shiny-shoed dork."

"No, Matt," said Lisa, grabbing his arm. "Let me call him."

"No. I'm speaking to him. I need to sort this out."

"Well, be honest with him, please, and don't get all blokey."

"I'll be honest with him," said Matt. "Just enjoy your champagne, and I'll be back in five minutes."

Charlie looked up, wide-eyed, as she continued to order what sounded like squid in aniseed and grilled pork intestines while Matt left to speak to Peter.

"Hard to see how this is going to end well," Lisa said to Max.

"Maybe I should fill your glass?" he offered, and they raised their champagne in a mini toast.

Charlie finished ordering as Matt came back.

"All done," he said, giving Lisa her phone.

"And...?" said Lisa. "What did he say?"

"He promised to keep away from you."

"What? Really? Just like that?"

"Well, when I threatened to break him into tiny pieces, he said he'd keep away."

"Matt! You can't threaten him."

"Can't I?"

"No - he's a lawyer. He'll come after you with a legal writ or something."

"Good for him, and I'll go after him with a baseball bat or something."

"No, Matt. I thought you were going to talk to him. I didn't realise you were going to threaten violence."

Matt shrugged. "I was just honest with him like you asked me to be. I promised that - in all honesty - if he came near you, I would kill him."

"OK. Let's have a toast," said Charlie, eager to dissipate the argument. "Let's raise our glasses to Lisa and Matt."

"Lisa and Matt," echoed Max, while Matt leaned over and kissed Lisa lightly on her cheek.

"You've got to see the funny side," said Charlie, taking a large sip of her drink. "You thinking that Matt was having an affair with a woman old enough to be his mother. And Matt and Peter both dashing here after you. It *is* quite amusing."

"It's not at all amusing," said Lisa.

"Yeah, it is," said Charlie. "It's actually really amusing."

"You know what...I've had a thought," said Lisa.

"Well, it had to happen one day," Max quipped as Lisa nudged him fondly and ignored the comment.

"Why don't you both come back to Cove Bay? Come to the Ball, and meet all the players. My sisters would love to see you, and I bet your mum's dying to see the two of you."

"I'm in," said Max. "Will the rich lady be there?"

"It's in Nancy's house, of course; she'll be there," said Lisa.

"You know, that's a really good idea," said Charlie. "I'd love that."

"Great news," said Matt.

"Yay!" said Charlie, hugging Lisa. "I'm coming back to Cove Bay!"

CHAPTER 21

"*A*re we sure about this?" said Charlie, as Isabella's assistant put extensions into her hair, curling them and pinning them up, making her look like a Hollywood star. "It's like I stepped out of the 1920s. Is this a good look? Are we sure? I need some proper advice...where's Sophia?"

"Just relax," said Lisa. "Your hair looks perfect. Sophia will be here soon. We're going to a ball in a gorgeous mansion, not some hip Edinburgh joint. You're supposed to look dreamy and romantic, not cutting-edge cool. You look perfect."

"Mmmm...I guess," said Charlie, entirely unconvinced.

She was enjoying the pampering, though. Even though she lived in Edinburgh with beauty spas and hairdressers on every street corner, she never had any time to enjoy them. It was lovely to come here and relax. That's what she missed about Cove Bay; everything was so calm and peaceful, and everyone was so friendly. Perhaps she should come back permanently? Her mum would love it if she did.

THE WOMEN all got dressed at home in a collection of gowns supplied by Sophia's boutique. Isabella had brought her assistant hairdressers in, and make-up artists were in attendance to ensure the girls looked better than they had ever looked before.

Charlie was ready first, in a beautiful, black, elegant, long evening dress. She looked lovely with white gloves that reached her elbows and brought images of Audrey Hepburn to mind. "You look so stylish and gorgeous," said Lisa, looking at her friend with pride. "Lovely. I hope someone gorgeous and fantastic sweeps you off your feet tonight; then you might stay in Cove Bay, and we'll all be together again."

"It's been a long time since any sweeping me off my feet took place, but let's hope!" she said, giving a little twirl. "I love this dress so much."

Lisa's mom wore a traditional '50s-style prom dress, with a beautiful tulle ballerina skirt that swung out in a perfect soft-blue colour. It was a replica of the one she had worn at prom, where she met her husband all those years ago.

"How on earth did you find this dress?" asked Georgina. "It's wonderful and exactly like the one I wore years ago. I love it. Thank you, angel."

"I took the picture of you out of the photo album and got it made," said Sophia. "I knew you'd look amazing in it. It's like you haven't aged a day."

Sophia looked beautiful, of course, in the most elegant white dress. If Lisa had worn a white dress, there would have been red wine all down it within about ten minutes, but everyone knew that Sophia would return looking as gorgeous and immaculate as she left. It was a beautiful, form-fitting dress that was very Marilyn Monroe. There was no doubt that the entire North Carolina Sharks team would be gathering around her tonight.

Emma had kept her outfit casual, predictably enough. She and Sophia looked like they were going to entirely different parties, as Emma could only be persuaded to wear a black pair of silk trousers and a flattering emerald-green top. She looked lovely, of course, because she was so pretty, but it was a shame they couldn't get her more dressed up. Sophia had given her the most beautiful velvet ankle boots to wear with her trousers, to extend her legs and give her that flash of glamour that the others all had, but Emma wasn't having any of it; she had slipped on a pair of flat shoes that would allow her to dance the night away.

Isabella looked lovely in a black-and-white striped dress. She was so worried about her weight all the time and so paranoid about being bigger than everybody else that she was determined stripes would make her look slimmer. They did—she looked lovely, elegant, and very Hollywood as she strolled through the living room and gave a twirl.

Lisa looked into the mirror again; it was her turn to go out, but she felt so self-conscious. She hadn't had as much time to get ready as the others because she'd been at the house all day, ensuring the gardens were perfect.

Now, here she was, dressed in pink. It wasn't a colour she usually wore, but she wanted to make an effort tonight. She heard the door-bell ring and the men arrive to pick them up; she heard them walk into the living room and knew she had to make her entrance. She stepped out of the bedroom and walked into the living room to gasps of appreciation. Matt stood up and walked toward her.

In his tuxedo, he looked incredible—so handsome, so lovely. He took her hand and kissed it, and she looked into his eyes.

"You look beautiful," he said as the others all shouted at her to give them a twirl. She moved into the centre of the room and turned slowly around. The breathtaking dress in a baby-pink colour, encrusted with the tiniest sparkling stones, looked like something that Cinderella would wear to the ball. Her hair had been put up, with tendrils dropping around her face. She wore tiny diamond studs in her ears that reflected the jewels all over her dress. She felt great. She looked at Matt and felt even better. She had a feeling that life ahead of her would be fantastic, and she couldn't wait to grab it and enjoy it.

WANT to know what happens next?
CLICK HERE TO FIND OUT My Book

In 'Girls At Sunshine Cottage' learn what happens to Matt and Lisa. Will they move to the big house together? What will become of their love?

*In the new story, you will also learn more about **Isabella**, the chatty hairdresser who's seen Lisa find love and would like to find someone like that for herself. But she is paranoid about her weight and convinced that no one will want her unless she gets slimmer. She turns to the Sharks players to ask for help and in walks Greg—all muscles and charm.*

While Isabella turns her attention to Greg, things seem to be going very wrong at the salon; clients get messages cancelling appointments, deliveries are all wrong and soon there are personal attacks. Is someone trying to hurt her by making it look like she is causing all the trouble? Who would possibly want to cause her pain?

With her sisters firmly by her side, she sets out to get to the truth behind the strange occurrences.

Along the way, the two men in her life fall under the spotlight. Could the trouble be caused by Andy the local plumber who pops in to see how she's doing, and keeps asking her out on dates? Or did she throw herself into the lions' den when she teamed up with Greg to try and get fit?

Isabella hopes not. She had her heart set on working with the fitness expert to lose lots of weight, and the plumber is soooo fanciable.

Or is it someone else? Perhaps someone who came into the salon?

Isabella has no idea, but she's determined to find out.

If you want to be on the mailing list for future books, competitions & other fun stuff, drop me an email at: **bernicenovelist@gmail.com.**

STAY IN TOUCH

WEBSITE:
Website: www.bernicebloom.com

SOCIAL MEDIA
Facebook: https://bit.ly/3iwKUOW
Twitter: https://bit.ly/3iv7NlO
Instagram:https://bit.ly/3nlBVUn

BOOKS ON AMAZON
Books on Amazon (US):
https://amzn.to/3cYuCwW
Books on Amazon (UK):
https://amzn.to/3lfPwui

Printed in Dunstable, United Kingdom

65908339R00099